EVENIN(

NUMBER 2, SPRING 2010

. . .all men and women are created equal.

> —Elizabeth Cady Stanton, revision of the
> American Declaration of Independence,
> 1848

PUBLISHED TWICE A YEAR
BY
EVENING STREET PRESS

EDITOR: Gordon Grigsby

ASSOCIATE EDITOR: Jan Schmittauer

MANAGING EDITOR: Barbara Bergmann

EVENING STREET REVIEW is published in the spring and fall of every year by Evening Street Press.   United States subscription rates are $24 for one year and $44 for two years (individuals), and $32 for one year and $52 for two years (institutions).

ISBN: 978-0-9820105-4-9

EVENING STREET REVIEW is centered on the belief that all men and women are created equal, that they have a natural claim to certain inalienable rights, and that among these are the rights to life, liberty, and the pursuit of happiness. With this center, and an emphasis on writing that has both clarity and depth, it practices the widest eclecticism.   EVENING STREET REVIEW reads submissions of poetry (free verse, formal verse, and prose poetry) and prose (short stories and creative nonfiction) year round. Submit 3-6 poems or 1-2 prose pieces at a time. Payment is one contributor's copy. Copyright reverts to author upon publication. Response time is 4 to 5 weeks. Please address submissions to Editors, 7652 Sawmill Rd., #352, Dublin, OH 43016-9296. Email submissions are also acceptable, and may be sent to the following address as attached Microsoft Word or RTF files: editor@eveningstreetpress.com.

The Press intends to reprint in its entirety the Helen Kay Chapbook Prize winning manuscript from the previous year in the Spring issue of the Review.

For submission guidelines, subscription information, selected works, and news, please visit our website at www.eveningstreetpress.com.

Cover image: Mulberry Street in New York City 1900 (Detroit Publishing Co.)

. . . my mother does not care for thought,
and father, too busy with his briefs to
notice what we do. He buys me many books,
but begs me not to read them, because he
fears they joggle the mind. They are
religious, except me, and address an eclipse
every morning, whom they call "Father."

> —Emily Dickinson: from a letter to Thomas
> Higginson, who'd asked about her family,
> April 1862

EVENING STREET REVIEW

PUBLISHED TWICE A YEAR BY EVENING STREET PRESS

NUMBER 2, SPRING 2010

CONTENTS

NONFICTION

FICTION

OCCASIONAL NOTES

THE PURSE SEINE

Our sardine fishermen work at night in the dark of the
      moon; daylight or moonlight
They could not tell where to spread the net, unable to
      see the phosphorescence of the shoals of fish.
They work northward from Monterey, coasting Santa
      Cruz; off New Year's Point or off Pigeon Point
The look-out man will see some lakes of milk-color light
      on the sea's night-purple; he points, and the helms-
      man
Turns the dark prow, the motorboat circles the gleaming
      shoal and drifts out her seine-net. They close the
      circle
And purse the bottom of the net, then with great labor
      haul it in.

             I cannot tell you
How beautiful the scene is, and a little terrible, then,
      when the crowded fish
Know they are caught, and wildly beat from one wall to
      the other of their closing destiny the phosphorescent
Water to a pool of flame, each beautiful slender body
      sheeted with flame, like a live rocket
A comet's tail wake of clear yellow flame; while outside
      the narrowing
Floats and cordage of the net great sea-lions come up to
      watch, sighing in the dark; the vast walls of night
Stand erect to the stars.

             Lately I was looking from a
      night mountain-top
On a wide city, the colored splendor, galaxies of light:
      how could I help but recall the seine-net

Gathering the luminous fish? I cannot tell you how beau-
      tiful the city appeared, and a little terrible.
I thought, We have geared the machines and locked all
      together into interdependence; we have built the
      great cities; now
There is no escape. We have gathered vast populations
      incapable of free survival, insulated
From the strong earth, each person in himself helpless,
      on all dependent. The circle is closed, and the net
Is being hauled in. They hardly feel the cords drawing,
      yet they shine already. The inevitable mass-dis-
      asters
Will not come in our time nor in our children's, but we
      and our children
Must watch the net draw narrower, government take all
      powers—or revolution, and the new government
Take more than all, add to kept bodies kept souls—or
      anarchy, the mass-disasters.

                  These things are Prog-
   ress;
Do you marvel our verse is troubled or frowning, while
      it keeps its reason? Or it lets go, lets the mood flow
In the manner of the recent young men into mere hys-
      teria, splintered gleams, crackled laughter. But they
      are quite wrong.
There is no reason for amazement: surely one always
      knew that cultures decay, and life's end is death.

                    —Robinson Jeffers
                    1937

PAULA ANNE YUP

CHILDHOOD

In looking back to those Phoenix years in the 50's, 60's and 70's
how it hurts like bad sunburn to remember myself as a Chinese girl
with parents who spoke English badly, we had very little to live on,
my father had a bad temper and I had a short skinny little body
and how could I keep clean when we had no hot water in the house?
I had to boil lots of water in big pots in our kitchen and carry heavy pots
with my matchstick arms to the bathtub. It took several trips and I'd
spill hot water on my feet and legs so it hardly seemed a bother to bathe
especially if my two little brothers would run into the room and out
laughing like they once did.

My three noisy brothers teased me endlessly and my sister yelled
because I got A's and she didn't. Who did she think I was?
Some doctor who could cure her from getting C's? How could I help?
It took all my energy to do my own work. If she was stupid
who could help that? At least she had my mother and father
at peace with her and all she had to do was not talk all day.
She managed my father when I couldn't no matter how I tried.

My father gave me grief over everything it seemed. Nothing of me
pleased him at all and how I tried. He loved the dramatic
to make a point with us noisy kids. He threw two of my brothers
right into the trash can once. Good riddance he said. Screamed.
How timid he made me when he molested me in the bedroom
with the TV on real loud while he helped me do math homework
when my mother was out of the house cashiering at a store
after our own small store bit the dust after the riots.
He also tried to strangle me once and my two brothers
burst into the room and pulled him off me. He gave them pushups.
And me, I guess I got my breath back.

So when I went to college I made good my escape from hot
sorrowful Phoenix full of bad memories I'd rather leave alone.
Later therapy showed me that no good came of my childhood.
This went on for decades, my past a painful boil which needed
lancing at the hands of some doctor. Some therapist maybe.

But this week when I felt sad over world events and I'd fret
watching the TV and feeling helpless sinking despair
while doing the laundry doing the dishes doing the shopping
I got childhood memories again. I remembered myself
a young girl scout in my brownies outfit and then my green
uniform and of meeting at Madrid Elementary School
and the sound of taps which made me sorrowful in a good way.

Then I thought of my thermos which my mother would put
Campbell's chicken noodle soup in and a sandwich
sans mayonnaise or lettuce for my lunch, or myself
next door playing billiards, or Mexican migrant workers
with lots of watermelons in the back of a beat up truck
for our store before it failed, or of how hot Phoenix got
and how cold the air conditioner made the library
in a shopping center, or of my best friend's house,
of going with my father to farms to look at puppies
or of my friends Emmett and Leesi coming to the store.

I could remember drinking wine with my dinner
when I visited my Italian friend although I didn't know
it was wine in grade school. I had a Navajo friend up the street
and how big her brothers and father who did construction work
seemed compared to me, my friend and her petite soft voiced mother.
The memories continued to spill over me as big waves
and I could see our German Shepherd dogs Lady and King
and our Chows Lim and Kim, then I'm at an Associated Grocers
Convention with my father looking at things for sale on display
and more memories continue to flood my life and my chores.

I can remember shoeshine boys and their little wooden boxes,
of the junkman pushing his cart through the streets, of meat
my brother and I got from the meat store a block away
from our store, of Mr.White the palest Black man we knew
who made us ice cream sundaes in his restaurant and his big
wraparound porch and house when we did deliveries.

Then I remember the suburbs again after the store failed
of my parents and us kids visiting my mother's coworker
at their shabby dirty little house and ranch but full of books

with dog hair and excrement on a floor none too clean
and the blessed outdoors with the horses in their corral
many more memories crowd each other out
so my childhood no longer seems cursed by my parents
loudly yelling at each other in village Cantonese
or tainted by my father's ridicule of me so tears
would run down my face as I'd sob till my muscles hurt.

More happened than the awful and painful past, a boil
too painful to touch. Sometimes I had fun too
like how I met the midgets up the street from our home
while trick-or-treating on Halloween. These circus guys
I could see straight into their eyes when they gave me candy.

NATALIA BARB

MAMMA

Teach us to make tortillas Mamma,
Por favor?
Si, mamma, *yes,* we know.
Please, Mamma?
How do we know how to roll
Our chocolate eyes so knowingly?
Like the rr in *burrito.*
Perhaps rolling tortillas would come just as easily,
As naturally, as if we were born to it,
But we will never know,
We must say "Yes,"
And no, we never roll tortillas.

We look at Mamma's tired hands,
We promise we would never be like her,
Scrubbing floors.
Mamma says
We will be the smart girls,
The college girls,
Never let that Espanola
Burn our tongues like poison.

We love to eat chiles,
But we do not hold their heat.
We do not have that cayenne in our blood,
No red desert earth in our skin;
Our skin est bonita.
Mullato.
Warm like atole,
Smooth.
We must never play in the sun,
Mamma says,
And wear long sleeves and floppy hats,
Better to look silly—
We do not want to turn brown like potatoes;
We do not want to

Turn dark.

Now we sit around talking loudly
Drinking coronas and margaritas
In the back yard,
Pretending to be Mexicanos,
Eating canned picante
And store-bought tortillas,
We remember our Mamma
With her calloused knees,
And we do not speak her Spanish
Nor roll our rr's.

MYLES GORDON

RECITE EVERY DAY

Winner of the Helen Kay Chapbook Prize, 2009 (printed complete here)

1

2008 - Massachusetts

The rabbi asks how she's doing with her soul
now that she's reached end stage cancer,
meaning: is she ready with God? She's pretty well
come to terms, I say. A passenger
like a Russian doll inside a Russian doll
arriving at the last one, finally.
What about you? the rabbi asks. I'm fine with it, and all
the rest of it at forty-seven is ancient history.

Skipping work to go to Costco, buying
her a high definition TV,
hooking it up, teaching her the clicker, crying
all the way to the car. Bullshit. History
is one teetering log from flooding in.
Here I am reliving it again.

2

1979 - Massachusetts

Sleeping bag, pup tent, extra clothes, back-pack stuffed,
water bottle hanging off the back,
wool socks, first aid, rain coat, more than enough.
Summer shimmer rising off the black
tar of Route 95, the guardrail's curve.
Gusts from semis. Holding my baseball cap
with one hand, thumb out with the other. Prayer: swerve
into the breakdown lane. Stop. Pick me up.

Eighteen, moved out the month before from the brother
with issues, Hustler magazines
and hands he couldn't keep off me, the father and mother
who didn't know but knew, monstrous scenes…
Standing, waiting in the northbound lane —
beyond escape, no other plan.

3

1932 - Massachusetts

Eight, strep throat blossoms to rheumatic fever,
two years convalescence Jewish Home
For Destitute Children in Dorchester, heart murmur
fluttering, syncopated metronome.
Useless joints, limbs, baby stroller
to get to appointments, or else in bed
waiting for the nurse who speaks Yiddish to tell her
no family visited today even though they said they would.

Midnight, a teenage boy trying to sneak
to   a teenage girl in my mother's ward, crawling
by her bed, startling her, whispering *go back
to sleep*. My mother scared, bawling
all night: *I want to go home, want to go home.*
No one, nothing could make her calm.

4

1968 - Massachusetts

Eight, alone with him all day then just alone.
Mother sleeping on the couch, night nurse.
In the basement, the record player on,
scratched forty-fives. Time to rehearse
one of the rituals, falling into his lap,
no, this way, his feet on my ass, letting go,
falling again and again but keep
doing it even though I don't want to.
Later in the kitchen by myself
with a sharp knife I'm not allowed to touch
pressing it both hands against my chest
mother still asleep on the couch.
Standing paralyzed in a silent terror
that a car horn shatters like a broken mirror.

5

1940 - Massachusetts

She throws the dishes then steps
in the cardboard carton, stomping with thick-
soled shoes, exploding shards with floral tips,
screaming at her husband in her thick
English Yiddish mixture what a failure he is,
that she doesn't want to move with
him again. The four daughters watching as
he leans, punching her in the mouth.
My mother, sixteen, walking through broken china, grabs
the kitchen knife, makes up her mind, starts
toward him, saying: *I swear I'll stab
you if you hit her again. I'll stab you in the heart.*
The six of them now quiet in the room.
Someone leaves to go and get a broom.

6

1976 - Massachusetts

At least a half a bottle of aspirin
I tell her. She drives me to the doctor.
No need to pump my stomach. No nausea, pain.
He takes me in alone, asks if I'd ever
thought of suicide before. I don't know
if I answer. He asks if I take drugs. My mother
in there with him now asks if I take drugs. No
to both of them. It's true, no matter
how they're looking at me, that's not why.
I can't tell them why – I'm so used to it.
I don't know what I tell them, if I lie,
or not. I tell them out of force of habit
in words that come out like a foreign language
hiding truth, anesthetizing damage.

7

2008 - Massachusetts

She opens a Bank of America account
after she moves to the new complex closer
to us, then decides to make it joint
so that as she falls apart with the cancer
we'll have access to her cash to help her shop
and pay for prescriptions, et cetera. We sit
with the matronly manager who takes us through each step –
a few clicks, it's done – the procedure to change it.
My mother tries to change her mind, afraid
the seventy five dollars the bank gave her to entice
her to open the first time would be null and void
if my name were added. The manager offers solace,
pats her hand, tells her: *don't worry.*
Nothing is going to happen to your money.

8

1965 - Massachusetts

My brother screaming he'll run away.
I call my mother stupid, tag behind him like I always do.
Outside, a change of plans, says he'll lay
in the street, get run over, I panic: *no!*
run back home trying to sputter to my mother,
as best as I can understand, what happened,
that I am so scared for my brother.
She slaps me mad as hell: *you called me stupid.*
I'm wavering in tears when he comes in,
puts down his suitcase, cries and goes to her.
Leaning to his reaching arms, embracing him,
she kneels. They sit cuddling on the floor.
All these years later, watching her nod off,
sick, on the couch: *enough resentment. Enough.*

9

1988 - Massachusetts

Sitting in a pizza parlor before
she and my father move to Florida
she asks me if I ever could forgive her.
No. That's a lie. She says she did a
bad thing not protecting me. A lie.
Truth, She asks me if I'm mad. That's all she'll give.
The truth is that she doesn't even try
to offer me a reason to forgive.
I sit there thinking how in just a week
they'll both be gone and I won't have to have
these awful talks with her, won't have to speak
to them again. Guilty, relieved,
I see her like a loyal subject, small and sad,
awaiting my decree. *No. I'm not mad.*

10

2008 - Massachusetts

CT Scan on computer screen, the tumor
hangs like a mushroom cloud caught in freeze frame,
roiling out its tendrils to consume her.
And, no, there isn't anyone to blame,
the fat end above her liver and the rest
in spidery spirals and thick black coil
like some toxic Rorschach test.
But standing here right now seems so disloyal:
the oncologist with her finger on the screen
running it along the grainy shot
as if touching something taboo and obscene
with us all watching her, and we're caught
poring over this intimate, awful image
as if tasting from the forbidden fruit of knowledge.

11

1930 - Poland

The petty terrors: ruffians on the street
burning a pig late Friday afternoon,
unclean smoke mixed with summer heat
sweeping through the village. They will finish soon,
at least lose interest, wander off to drink,
fire fading, a few hours of Shabbos peace.
Her mother trying to wave away the stink,
her grandparents cleaning.
             The pungent grease
gushing, flowering sores sprouting on blisters,
face charred black, the curved, scowling jaw,
swirling flies as each petal opens and festers.
At six, just one of the ugly things she saw.
Now eighty-four. I ask that when she dies
that moment doesn't flash before her eyes.

12

1930 - Poland

The drone of bees inside the splintered wood:
the men at evening prayer. The way they bowed
and undulated on the beats of every word
frightened her, the bits she understood
popped from undecipherable figure eight
of diagonal chant, voluminous monotone,
until she'd find a way to tune it out
and be inside that crowded room alone.
She thought of bees: the way at dusk they'd swarm
to the mound of brush pressed against the woodpile,
how from every direction they would come,
disappearing in a tighter and tighter spiral
into the wind flap of their papery hole
singing secret psalms and phrases of her soul.

13

1973 - Massachusetts

Seersucker coat, bowtie, baby fat
rolled from the collar, standing on the stage
in front of all of them, wondering what
I was doing there, feeling the rage
sink into fear, holding the silver hand
against the perfect parchment, letters clean,
immaculately drawn, having to stand
reciting words not knowing what they mean,
put Torah back and face the congregation
mumble through my sermon's awkwardness
finish my Bar Mitzvah coronation
with my parents' blessing (I confess,
I can't remember anything they said
and the only one who does will soon be dead.)

14

2008 - Massachusetts

Methadone: the word itself illicit
except it's her best shot to ease the pain.
She's hesitant. She doesn't want to risk it.
The hospice nurse comes over to explain
she won't become an addict: *at your dose
you won't be selling your body on the street
for your next fix.* My mother: *I suppose...
unless you can get me a lucrative corner.* A treat
to see her humor, even at her age,
the spinning cotton candy in her gut
splintering tumors taking her to the next stage,
cocoon completing end of story, but
three days into the drug she doesn't know
who I am. I tell her. She still doesn't know.

15

1977 - Massachusetts

Tissue paper Zig Zags, *White Album* open
nickel bag spread, separating seeds
onto the photo of George Harrison.
Lennon gets the good stuff. Righteous weed
on top of "Revolution Number Nine"
half the world asleep and half awake.
Seesaw eyelids open/close keeping time
with the rhythm of the planets. With the music.
Folding the album like a butterfly,
roll it, light it, toke before I lose it —
another teenage existential high.
Then realization. Someday the vases all will crack
the spilling souls unable to spill back.

16

1979 - Canada

Picked up by a trucker, six A.M.
beer belly sweaty shirt, two sizes tight,
bald middle-aged he asks how "big" I am.
C'mon, buddy, he pleads, put your hand on it
(we're buddies now). Too tired, I comply.
He looks and reaches but I turn too quick.
C'mon, I tell him back, *give me a ride*
or let me off, letting him know my prick
is off the map. Back toward him, I watch
the guardrail blur when I look sideways, clear
when I look straight up. I stare at my crotch
and feel him breathe behind my shoulder.
Three-hundred mile stalemate, stop at noon,
jump out, grab my pack, stick out my thumb.

17

2008 - Massachusetts

Panic: you're not opening your door
so building maintenance helps the nurse get in,
she and your aid finding you on the floor.
They call me. I arrive. No one knows when
the stroke happened. You sit. You seem to know
who we are but you can't talk. We lift
you in a blanket, carry you, slow,
to the bedroom. You're favoring your left
side. The right side of your face droops. We wait
for the hospital bed, the liquid methadone
for this next phase, and I know it's too late
to ask you anything anymore, what's unknown
will stay that way — and soon the time to grieve

after watching you lie there forgetting how to breathe.

18

2008 - Massachusetts

The mower by the open window stalls
the lecturer who stops and waits mid-sentence
until it passes, and the machine's roar falls
allowing her to continue on repentance
in Russian poetry. Later, my wife
calls to ask if it's okay that our son
tags graffiti on our newly painted garage. Life
continues her distractions, even when
I don't think I can take them anymore —
the cut grass on the sidewalk in a wave
wind-blown, messages streaked on the garage door,
the lecture's end, the dirt around your grave
less visible, delineations gone,
fresh planted grass seed sprouting, growing in.

19

2008 - Massachusetts

Circular stains on her last pillowcase,
landfill now? I don't remember what
we did with her bedding. Not a trace
of them remains, apartment, emptied out,
already leased to the next resident.
We want her taken out the front door
when the time comes, said the president
of the senior center. *The Golda Meir*
House has a policy. It's all a part of it.
So when they crossed her arms across her chest
and put her in the bag and rolled her out
and everybody knew that she was dead
I forgot the linens on her bed.

20

2008 - Massachusetts

I forgot the linens on her bed,
the blankets she last touched, the blue nightgown
she was wearing; no ritual funeral shroud,
spun in vast factories somewhere and found
in Walmart, Sears and K Mart, peasant cloth
from fluttering hands on stainless steel machines,
the kind her mother made, that no one with wealth
paid attention to, the era where kings and queens
and Czars all went from immortal to mortal,
palaces broken open spilling out
their treasures, broken porcelain, the colossal
wreck of revolution, every rout
leading to the horror of world war
dead buried in whatever it was they wore.

21

1969 - Massachusetts

You made the burger rare, the way I liked,
between two white bread slices, crusts cut off,
juice and ketchup bleeding through each piece,
and let me eat on the porch. It was enough
for happiness. Fingertips wet and greasy,
I sat with my plastic cup of milk,
plate balanced on my knees, the evening easy
and rising from the tight-wound hinge and click
of my family's trappings into sparkling days
where the waves fell silent and I became another
boy who wanted to feel like this always,
bringing my cup and plate back to my mother.
Suddenly offered now from memory's pantry —
quick – gobble it before it goes away.

22

1973 – Massachusetts

Nightshift nurse, you slept on the couch during the day
and I was of the age and curious.
You wore a long skirt. This is the way
I remember it. You had turned your face
into the couch's rough cloth, lips brushing the checkered pattern
as I brushed your ankle, lifting the hem, pulling up,
fingertip running slowly across the nylon
until I reached your knee and stopped.
Three days before you died, after your stroke,
when I helped you to the bathroom from your bed,
your legs blue through paper skin, I had to look,
in order to clean and change you, where I once had
turned away. A streetcar stops outside.
The passengers spill out of it like blood.

23

2008 – Massachusetts

My brother came three days before you died
and screamed he had the right to be in charge
even though your legal papers said
I was the sole health proxy. In his rage
a familiar echo. Family gct together
some aunt's house, a five and dime magic trick
he wanted to show; me, the mischievous brother
giving away the secret, the sick
retaliation. Here, screaming like he did
then at the sibling injustice of it all,
a two-hundred fifty pound jealous kid
because I was the one that hospice called.
In the final hours before you died
I was six years old again, no place to hide.

24

1968 – A Vision

A woman in babushka sitting
on the edge of my bed, stroking my head
as I woke, or was I dreaming?

Gently the soul slumbers, she said.

Thick strawberry red hair, quiet face,
she appeared one night
as if breaking the surface

of dark, still water: *we know your plight.*

Forty years later, I
remember waking that morning the first time in ages
not even wanting to die.
Oh Sages,

Oh Mother of Blessed Memory,
answer me, please answer, who was she?

25

2008 - Massachusetts

What happens when a soul in passing passes?
Is it like the anchor of a relay team
taking the baton? Or slow and serious,
creeping night by night in a serial dream
dreamed by the living but forgotten in
the morning? Or is it more how you believed –
that there is no spirit? And is it a sin
to now think there is? And maybe I shouldn't have grieved –
that's something you wouldn't want – so you made sure
by living on the cheap, thrift stores, et al,
to leave something that would make us feel secure
which turned out to be not very much at all
especially if banking on big annuities
and a windfall of 4.5 percent CDs.

26

1930 – Poland

A strong wind. The smoke bows to its knees,
grandparents charging the wagon, *bubbe* yells
take care of the children! You want to freeze
the moment, you want to cast one of those spells
of which Jews are accused, make the distances
between you and them constant, a steady tug of thread
no one but you can see: the entrances
into their hearts. Now all of you dead.

Sixty years later, when I visit Yad Vashem
they check the files and data base
against the Xeroxed, scrawled postcards with each name
in Yiddish, looking up with *sorry, no trace*
as the government told your mother years ago.
Now, at the end of the fraying thread, you know.

27

1930 – Poland

Now, at the end of the fraying thread, you know
the pattern of the seam stitched by the rails…
Pre-dawn after the wagon ride, so
tired that the whistles from the trains
were like distant thunder in a summer storm
even though they were on top of you. You boarded
with your mother and sisters, sat on
wooden seats in the back, departed.
Watching the blur of trestles out the window
you thought if you could only remember each turn
and twist some day you'd come home again. No.
The juncture, all those confusing tracks, there'd be no return –
watching your life unravel where you couldn't follow,
you unraveled from the inside, scooped hollow.

28

2008 – Massachusetts

Our cat ran off a week before you died.
My wife forgot to close the kitchen screen
after handing a toy out to our son. She cried.
She knew that I would yell and make a scene.
I did. Stayed up half the night, the back door open,
put out a dish filled with tuna the color of
a child's pink eraser torn.
Didn't touch her when I went to bed. Love
frays like yarn. Friday, before you died,
I helped you with your air conditioner.
You asked if things were alright
between me and Jody. I told you of course they were.
I saw the cat in the yard beneath the full moon.
I inched outside. She ran.

29

2008 – Massachusetts

I'm supposed to recite Kaddish every day
for a year. I managed a week,
tallit, teffilin. Golem of clay,
rise from the marshes, speak
the names of the dead
so that they may stand beside you.
Speak the whispered name of G-d.
Beloved Sarai, who
welcomes all to the tent,
welcome me and welcome Siossa, your daughter.
Allow us to repent,
allow us teshuvah.
She, for not being here,
I for failing her the year.

30

1930 – Poland

The small port in France you made it to the ship,
rowed out on the dinghy, had to climb
the spider web ladder, squares of blistering rope,
those beneath you pushing your behind,
you terrified and everywhere the salt spray.
Don't look down, they said so you looked up
at clouds unfolding minefield silver gray,
hands stinging red by the time you reached the top.
I always meant to ask what port that was,
the name of the ship, how long it took to cross,
what time of year, what kind of constant noise
the engines made. Instead I have the froth
of steamed milk in latté pressed against my lip
at Starbucks as I conjure your savior ship.

31

2002 – Massachusetts

Sitting watching *The Godfather Part Two*
on our couch, my wife between us,
my mother and I recite lines seconds before they do
on screen, Jody wondering what kind of family is this?
That Michael, he just went bad, my mother says
when he chastises poor Fredo on the lounge,
foreshadowing the awful thing he does.
Not when my mother's alive, Don Michael warns
his hit man, but when she dies, Fredo's fair game –
waiting, then, for his mother to die,
so he can kill his brother — all families the same
in flesh, in film, in poetry.
I sit alone in Starbucks wondering how
to let my brother go. *You're nothing to me now.*

32

1930 – Poland

You left at night, the grey chimney smoke
from the houses silhouette in moonlight
winding like a *minyan*. Clattering spokes
from the wagon, donkeys pulling, tight
yank on the reins, you, your sisters and mother
packed in with the hay, woolen blankets
around your shoulders. Your father in America
two years to raise the money. A few trinkets
in a duffel bag: rolled up paintings, candlesticks,
a silver watch, coins sewn in the flaps,
wool stockings, bolts for sewing, scarves and skirts.
Your grandmother calls. The wagon stops.
The outline of the village through waving trees.
A strong wind. The smoke bends and vanishes.

GLOSSARY

GOLEM – A creature of Jewish folklore— a man made of clay and brought to life

KADDISH – A prayer of mourning, praising God

MINYAN – The quorum necessary to recite certain prayers, consisting of ten adult Jewish men

SARAI – A name for Sarah, wife of Abraham. She and Abraham were both renowned for hospitality

TALLIT – A shawl-like garment worn during morning services

TEFILLIN – Phylacteries: leather pouches containing scrolls with passages of scripture

ADAM STURTEVANT

IN YOUR DREAMS

My friend Antoinette is one of those people who believes that everything you see in your dreams reveals a certain secret quality of your psyche. At the coffee shop where we work I mentioned to her that I had a recurring dream. Her eyes lit up, as if I'd been given a gift that she envied. I didn't want to get into the details with her, but she came over to my apartment after work and brought this book called, "Dream Symbology." It looked like a dictionary. It was just a long alphabetical list of objects and what they mean if you see them in your dream. Antoinette believes in stuff like this. She believes in astrology and astral projection. She does not believe in things like showering every day or shaving her armpits. She wears two crystals around her neck which she says harness good energy from Saturn and repel negative energy from Mars, respectively. If I ask too many questions about it, she drones on and on, so I hold my tongue about what I really think about giant gaseous planets sending their undetectable energies through thousands of light-years of space to influence the outcome of her job interviews. I don't tell her that her dread locks and tattered clothes carry significant influential energies of their own.

We sat on the carpet in my living room and leafed through the book. I couldn't believe how big it was.

Running: To run in your dream indicates anxiety. Running towards someone or something suggests great desire and apprehension. To run away from something suggests fear.

Elephant: To see an elephant in your dream is a sign that a distant memory is coming back to you, and must be addressed.

"Aren't these kind of obvious?" I said to Antoinette.

"Well, maybe those ones are, but there's tons of them— stuff you'd never think of. Listen to this:"

Volcano: A volcano in your dream is a sign that a great change is coming in your life, either geographical or emotional.

Pancakes: To eat pancakes in your dream shows that you are in need of love and sweetness, either from your family or significant other.

Speech: To give a speech in your dream shows that you have problems communicating with those around you.

It annoyed me that every entry contained the phrase, "in your dream." Wouldn't that get tiresome after a few hundred entries? I flipped through the book myself.

Underwater: To be underwater in your dream indicates that you are overwhelmed with your life's obligations.
Naked: To be naked in a public place in your dream suggests a fear of your secrets being exposed to those around you.

"So, basically, every dream is about being afraid, or inadequate, or unsatisfied with something," I said.

"God, Murphy, why are you such a buzzkill all the time?" She got up and grabbed her bowl and a bag of weed from her purse. "NO! Not every dream is about being afraid. Some of them are littler things, like being horny, or wanting to travel, or having a crush on somebody."

"I dreamt one time about being a character on Seinfeld. I'm pretty sure it was because I watched about a hundred episodes of Seinfeld that week."

"Maybe not. Look up 'Seinfeld.'" She giggled and packed the bowl.

"They're just so obvious. I could have written this book myself."

"Well, if it's so obvious, that makes it wrong? Doesn't that make it more…right?" She took a puff from the bowl and passed it to me. Maybe that's why I like hanging out with Antoinette, because we're such opposites that we reach some kind of equilibrium when we're together.

She asked about my dream and I told her some other time. I asked her to leave the book with me, and she agreed, but not without giving me that 'I told you so,' smile. After she left I was stoned and alone, the equilibrium vanished, and I began hating the book, so simple and arrogant there on the coffee table. It was the simplicity that bugged me, and the title, "Dream Symbology," the suffix claiming it to be a science, as if it's all been tested in clinical studies, as if Columbia University rounded up one hundred people who had dreamt of water buffalos, one hundred people who had not, and one hundred people who thought they remembered dreaming of water buffalos, but couldn't be entirely sure, and followed them around for a month afterwards, following their every move and every word, all the while subjecting each dreamer to rigorous psychological profiling. And what about all the combinations of things? What about an elephant underwater? What about eating pancakes naked in a volcano?

I leafed through it some more. With Antoinette gone, I could look up what I wanted.

Father: To see your father in your dream suggests that you are in need of guidance.
Death: To die in your dream, or see a loved one die, suggests that you fear for your own safety, or that of your loved one. To see a deceased person in your dream suggests that their memory (or spirit, depending on your beliefs) is surfacing (or making contact.)
Recurring: A recurring dream indicates an influence by its content so strong that it will continue to affect your life until it is addressed. Consider talking to a qualified psychologist, or (depending on your beliefs) a spiritual advisor.

For most of my life I didn't remember my dreams after waking up, unless I thought they were so funny or weird I had to tell somebody. But usually they were less funny when I retold them. I once dreamt of an outdoor fair for monsters and horror movie characters. Asleep, I thought it was brilliant that the slip-and-slide was for the skinless people from Hellraiser. I dreamt of a father waiting up all night for his disobedient teenage daughter to come home. When the tearful girl finally came through the door, she was ten feet tall and dressed in yellow armor, taken advantage of by her evil boyfriend who was bent on taking over the world by creating an army of giants.

Like every little boy I loved scary movies and was tormented by nightmares. But it wasn't the knife-wielding murderers or fanged monsters that plagued me. It was the grotesquely ill, bedridden mother in Pet Semetary, with the protruding vertebrae and gruel dripping from her mouth. It was the little girl in the Exorcist, with the deformed face and evil voice, tied to the bed in the other room of my house. I remember the part of the movie when the mother said to the priest, "That *thing* upstairs…" It wasn't the girl or the bedridden mother that scared me but the *thing* that had afflicted them both. Something invisible crept into the house undetected and slowly, gradually changed a person, bit by bit, stripping her of her humanity until nothing but the *thing* remained. My worst nightmares were those of proximity. I was most terrified of the thing not face to face with it, but somewhere else in the house, knowing it was just in the other room.

Monster: To see a monster in your dream suggests that you feel weak and overpowered by the forces in your life which scare you.
Illness: To experience an illness in your dream, or the illness of a loved one, suggests that the relationships with those around you need mending.

My father was afflicted with the thing, even before any of us saw the signs. He was always in the other room, never face to face with my mother or me. After work he would retire to the basement to work on his model airplanes and sip his screwdriver with classic rock on the radio. My mother explained to me early on that he liked to relax after work, which meant, "don't bother him." I did my best to obey. In the back corner of the basement was the spare refrigerator where we kept cases of soda. We developed an unspoken routine, him and I. On my trips downstairs to get a coke, I would pass by him at his worktable. Without looking up from his model, he would raise his right hand in the air and I would slap it and continue on. For many years, our father-son bonding was made up mostly of the no-look high-five.

It wasn't enough for me of course. One time, jolted by a sugar high, I lingered in the basement and sipped my coke. My father's head was bent close to his work in concentration. I danced to the music, and then lifted my arms out to my side and started spinning in a circle. The room blurred, my father's hunched back whizzed past my eyes, the music got alternately louder and softer. I lost myself in giddy pleasure. I unknowingly drifted closer to him as I spun, and I lost my balance. I fell into his back, snapping a tiny plastic tailpiece and spilling his drink. "God-DAMNIT, Billy!" is what he said. I cried, my mother lectured me, and the soda was moved to the upstairs kitchen.

When I arrived at the coffee shop the next day, Antoinette was already vibrating with caffeine and THC. I put my backpack in the back room and put on my apron. I started making myself an espresso.

"So?" she said, red eyes wide, and a hand on her hips.

"So? So what?" I said, sipping my drink.

She leaned in close to me and whispered, "Did you have *the dream* last night?"

I was caught off-guard by the question and looked back towards my backpack, as if I'd forgotten the dream somewhere inside it.

"Oh, I don't remember. I don't think so. I think I dreamt about making a speech naked at a waffle convention."

"Oh, really? Well, we must consult the book later. I'm pretty sure that's a good sign for your future."

"Nah, I looked it up already. Apparently, I'm petrified of spilling syrup on my penis."

"Hmm, that sounds yummy," she giggled. A customer was getting impatient at the counter, so she raced over, as if called to the stage. She had that unshakeable niceness with the customers, no matter how irate they got, as if she could convince them all they were being silly with her smile. All they saw were her red eyes and dreadlocks, but all she saw was the invisible beams from Saturn raining down through the ceiling, filling them all with purpose. Later, she chastised me for being too rough and careless when filling the tea bags.

"Mankind has been drinking tea for thousands of years. It's an ancient tradition, meant to lift our spirits and bring inner peace and wisdom," she said. I nodded, knowing there was more to come. "So you must be aware and respectful when you make the tea. The energy you put into the preparation is infused in it. If you slam the mug on the counter like an ogre, it'll taste like shit. Put a little love in it. Like this."

She showed me how gently she spooned out the leaves and carefully filled and folded the bag. "Always look them in the eye when you hand it to them too. You can make someone fall in love with you if you hand them a hot cup of tea the right way."

"I heard that ruffies work well, too."

"Ugh. You are such an Aries."

At first I rebelled and made the tea quickly. There were too many customers waiting in line for her coffee shop mysticism. I explained to her, though silently and in my mind, all the reasons why tea was tea, the only factors being how much and how hot. People are cranky for many more reasons than how their drinks are prepared, I told her. Not everything is cured with a wish and a warm look. People are not so simple. I snuck glances at her as she gleefully worked, dancing between the counter and shelf. "Good morning!" she sang. "How can I *help* you?" "What would you *like?*" I watched the customers' reactions, and they smiled back. "Enjoy!" she chirped as she handed them the mugs. Then Antoinette would catch my eye with that "I told you so" smile.

I was getting tired of her silence and her smirk, so I humored her and made the tea like a geisha for the rest of the day, handing it to the bleary-eyed yuppies with a smile. She watched over my shoulder as I scooped the tea, put her hand gently on my back, and said, "Good." I mimicked her enthusiasm as I took their orders. I didn't want to admit it, but it was kind of calming. For a moment it seemed like all I had to do was pretend to be happy, and it would evolve and mimic the real thing.

After the morning rush, I felt refreshed. The mood stayed with me. In a moment of warmth I said to Antoinette, "I looked through the book last night."

"Yeah? And?"

"It said I need either a psychologist or a spiritual advisor."

She grinned in a gesture of knowing.

"I obviously can't afford a psychologist."

She bent close and whispered.

"I can help you. But you'll have to tell me about your dream."

"Alright. Come over tonight after work," I said in surrender. "We'll need a lot of weed."

The thing that had infected my father gradually made itself known throughout the house when I was in high school. We avoided seeing it face to face as long as we could, but we were always aware of it the next room. It peeked out the windows every day when I came home from school. It filled the house with its silence, and later with its fray. He lost his job and stayed home with his airplanes, aircraft carriers and his drink. He changed in gradual steps, much like the girl in The Exorcist, but unlike her, he did not submit to doctor's visits or counseling. He refused.

In one of my most terrifying childhood Exorcist nightmares, I was locked in the room where the demon girl was detained. It was a tiny, dark room with narrow slotted walls. She didn't attack me or spin her head around or spray me with projectile vomit. We just sat across from each other and on a small table between us sat a greasy half-chewed roasted chicken, ostensibly what her caregivers gave her to eat.

Chicken: To see a chicken in your dream is a sign of cowardliness.

We didn't say anything to my father until it was too late. He was fired for drinking on the job, and was granted the new position of full-time alcoholic. His other habits faded. His models remained in pieces on the worktable. The bottle of glue hardened into rock. We needed an exorcist, but unlike the demon-girl, he did not welcome the challenge. Whether the talks were calm and rational or violent and tearful, he was unflinching in his order to leave him alone. I stayed out of the basement. A few months later, my worst nightmares had come true. In the very next room to mine, the thing lay confined to a white hospital bed and we were told to wait three weeks for it to die.

Antoinette came over that night and brought a black satin bag of crystals, incense and candles. She dimmed the lights and lit the candles, then packed a big bowl of weed. She seemed to be blossoming at this invitation, as if she'd done it before. We sat on the carpet and I took a big hit off the bowl, then another.

"So you're sure you're a qualified spiritual advisor?" I asked.

"Absolutely. I'm a Sagittarius, which means I'm acutely aware of people's energies. Plus, I've dated four Aries', so I'm pretty much an expert on your type. I know you better than you know yourself."

"Is that right?"

"Yes, that's right. I know you're skeptical, but obviously you're interested enough to ask for the book and invite me over, so first and foremost, you've got to stop pretending if we're going to make any progress." There it was: the equilibrium taking hold, congealing with the weed and candlelight. The room shrunk and morphed into a cocoon, and I was a grubby larva. I tried to remember that moment in the coffee shop, when she was right and I was wrong. I wanted to be more like her, to emerge from this a butterfly.

"Okay. I will stop pretending," I said.

"Good. Now tell me about your dream."

In the dim smoky haze of my apartment, after giving a brief background account of my father, I told Antoinette of my recurring dream. In it, I was in the backyard of my parents' house, and there were lots of people over for a party. All my friends from high school and all my parents' friends were there, talking and eating. The back door opens, and my father comes out, sickly yellow, drooling and gaunt, like in the final weeks. It was not taking place before he died, it was after and I remembered everything. He slowly stumbles outside and limps among the crowd. No one seems to notice. I start screaming at him, and then at my mother, screaming as loud and hard as I could, but they ignore me. I am screaming, "I thought you were dead! I thought he was dead! What happened?" I somehow remember that we had all thought he died, but it turned out to be a false alarm, and we were still waiting, and this makes me scream more.

Antoinette was quiet, and we looked at each other as if suddenly realizing how stoned we were, as if we'd made a mistake somewhere, as if we were doing this all wrong. I didn't want to, but I laughed.

"That one isn't in the book," I said.

She reached for it and cleared her throat. "Everything is in the book," she told me.

Resurrection: To see a deceased person alive again in your dream signifies that there is something you want to ask them or something you want to tell them, or (depending on your beliefs) that their spirit is trying to make contact.

"I don't think that this particular dream means that your father is trying to make contact," she says.

"How do you know?"

"Because if it was his spirit, he wouldn't be sick, he'd be healthy. Spirits don't get sick."

"Makes sense."

"But seeing him, and screaming...I think there's something you want to tell him."

"You think I'm a bad person."

"No, I do not. Why would I think that?"

"Because I see my father, and I want him dead."

"But he *is* dead," she feels bad saying. "How could that make you a bad person?"

"Because it was a relief when he died."

Before she left, she pulled a book about crystals from her bag and consulted it. The orange glow around my coffee table felt less like a cocoon. I was an even grubbier larva, drying out and crusting over. She told me that she was going to give me crystals to wear while I slept. Their energies would stimulate clarity, understanding, and spiritual growth. She also told me to start keeping a dream journal and write down everything I remember as soon as I woke up, and to consult the book. I would keep having the dream, but it would change. Things would be different. She took two crystals out of her bag, one red and one purple, and carefully put them in a small satin pouch on a string. She smiled and looked me in the eyes when she handed it over.

Alone and stoned, the candles and incense extinguished, the equilibrium gone, I regretted everything I told her. I had ruined her simple, beautiful view of the world. I had scribbled black marker over the pages in her books. I had ended the mystery she had liked about my dream. I had made everything ugly. I hated the book and the crystals on my coffee table, and I hated myself for hating them. I wanted that feeling back I had in the coffee shop, when I thought for a moment I could be more like Antoinette. I could grow my hair long and smile when I served tea and wear crystals that made me change. I put the pouch around my neck and searched for a pad and pen to put by my bedside table.

That night I dreamt of Antoinette. In the dream, I ran to her in the coffee shop, and frantically told her about the dream I had the night before. I was hyper and talking quickly, gesturing with my hands, illustrating in the air the effect that the crystals had had, how they had rescheduled the party at my parents' house, how it had bought us more time. She solemnly looked up to the chalkboard menu on the wall, consulting what type of tea I was supposed to drink after having had such a dream. Jasmine, she declared. She lit candles on the counter and dimmed the lights. The customers gathered round and watched patiently. She carefully brought down the jar of jasmine, and tenderly scooped it into the tea bag, and poured the hot water over. She looked in my eyes and reminded me that jasmine is a 'kiss tea,' so she gently pecked my lips before handing me the mug.

Dream: To dream or talk about a dream inside a dream is one of the rarest dream symbols. It signifies a period of self-reflection and deep thought. A dream within a dream within a dream is also possible, but usually only under the guidance of a spiritual advisor.

What I regretted most about that night with Antoinette was what I said about the relief I felt when my father died. It slipped out and was left hanging in the air like an unanswered question. What I didn't explain to her was how dense the thing had become in the house, invading every moment. My father was already gone, and all that was left was foul, concentrated suffering in a bed. I assumed that the thing would be gone when he died, but I was wrong. It lingered. Instead of grief, my mother had anger; she blamed him entirely. She would talk about him only with resentment—resentment for not trying, for refusing help, for forcing us to take care of him while we watched him die. The counselors called it a disease, but she called it something else. I hated the sound of her voice at those times, so I stopped bringing it up. We stopped talking about him, and in less than a year she had a new boyfriend. The thing festered in the other room.

Scream: To scream at someone in your dream indicates a reserve of long-suppressed anger towards someone close to you.

"Nothing yet," I said when I saw Antoinette at the coffee shop a couple days later.

"No change in the dream, or no dreams at all?"

"No dreams at all."

"It's okay. Sometimes it takes a while," she said. I knew she'd react that way, unsurprised. "Just keep wearing the crystals. They're working, even if you don't realize it."

I made an effort to serve the tea and coffee carefully and gracefully that day, but she didn't seem to notice. I couldn't shake the idea that she felt different about me since that night, or maybe different about herself. I resolved to be zenlike, and greeted the customers with a smile. Antoinette remained tired and distant.

"What's up with you? Rough night? Bad dreams?" I said.

"As a matter of fact, yes. I didn't sleep well."

"I never asked what you dream about. I assume you travel on flying crystals to Saturn and Mars to converse with your spirit animal? What was it again? A gerbil?"

"Actually, Smartass, I don't dream like most people. I practice lucid dreaming. Every night before bed, I visualize myself flying, and then I try to fly in my dream."

"Really? What's that like?"

"Exhausting."

I saw on the bulletin board near the entrance a flyer for the local movie theater. They were showing a new version of The Exorcist, with never-before-seen deleted scenes and special effects. Exorcist 2000 they were calling it. Instead of the usual promotional shot of the silhouette of the priest standing outside the house in the fog, there was a shadowy red picture of the girl's menacing face. I asked Antoinette if she wanted to go. She said she hadn't seen it and that she hated horror movies. I told her that it was the best horror movie ever made, that it was one of my favorites. I even told her that it had "spiritual overtones." Eventually she agreed. A customer at the counter asked to be helped, raising his voice to make his annoyance known.

"Yes! Yes, sir! What would you like?" she snapped.

I made myself some jasmine tea while she served him.

"God! Snapping at customers and seeing horror movies. I think you're rubbing off on me, Murphy," she said.

I raised my mug of tea.

"I think we're rubbing off on each other."

I hadn't seen The Exorcist in years. That, combined with the pot, wracked my nerves a little on the way to the theater. the effect it had on Antoinette. I wondered if it was reall t, or if my nightmares had given me a special vulnerability to it. My heart skipped a beat when the signs of possession started appearing: the peeing on the carpet, the ouija board, the doctor's visits. I looked over at Antoinette. She jumped at certain points and grabbed my arm with wide eyes and clenched teeth. Towards the end she seemed deep in thought.

I wasn't as scared as I thought I would be. I noticed all the little things that had been inserted that weren't in the original version: the fleeting images of the demon's face and the African statue. They appeared randomly in the house, unnoticed by the characters, just to startle us. To me, they ruined the movie. I thought about all the mystery and doubt in the original version, how no one really believes it's possession until the very end. Everyone has their own theory about hallucinations, seizures, neurological disorders, psychic powers. The doubt is what causes the suspense. In the original, no one is absolutely convinced until the girl levitates during the exorcism at the end. It's the not knowing that kills you. Those fleeting images declared right away the cause of the thing, and it cheapened the movie.

I explained all this to Antoinette on our walk back to my apartment. I talked and talked, passionately making a case for why the original was so much better. She listened silently, and I realized I was ranting.

"Sorry. I really think it's a great movie. It scared the shit out of me when I was little, but now, I just think it's a really great movie, maybe *because* I was so scared by it. I don't know. What did you think?"

"I see what you mean. It is a good movie. It's not like most horror movies. It's not just a monster chasing and killing people."

"I know!"

We continued our conversation back at my place over a fresh bowl of pot.

"It's actually very spiritual, I think," she said.

"See that? There's something in it for everyone. Even crystal-gazers."

"The whole thing about good versus evil. I mean, I'm not Christian or anything, but it was a real message I think. That one conversation between the priests summed up the whole thing."

"Which conversation?"

"When they're on the stairs, and the young priest asks the older priest why it was happening, why the demon targeted the innocent little girl. The older priest says, 'She's not the victim. We're the victims. He attacks the love we have for her.'"

I nodded and puffed on the bowl. I was glad she understood, and I was filled with a warmth for her. I wanted to somehow explain how it all related to my nightmares about my father, but it wouldn't make sense in words the way it did in my head. She went on.

"I think the scariest part is when she starts speaking in her own voice, the little girl voice, and she's saying, 'Help me.' Ugh! That was the worst! Because you hate the demon so much, but then you get a glimpse of the girl underneath, and you feel for her."

I felt my head swim. Something she said carried me back to those last few months, right before my father lost his job. As his drinking got more reckless, his personality changed. He started talking. He called me down to the basement. He sat at his worktable and pulled up a chair for me. With glazed-over eyes and a blissful look, he showed me his models. They were all planes from World War II, he explained. The B-17 Boeing Flying Fortress, the P-38 Lockhead Lightning, the P-39 Bell Air Cobra, the B-24 Consolidated Liberator. Then, the German planes: the Messerschmitt, the Heinkel, the Junkers. He explained each one's importance in the war, their particular uses, their strengths and weakness, the battles that were decided by each. He described the world that we might have lived in if the war was won by the other side. He showed me how the models came in so many pieces, how carefully he had to keep track of each piece, how if a single component was lost or broken, the model was lost. He told me how he had loved models when he was a kid. It was his father, my grandfather, who had bought him his first one and sparked his interest in the "hardware of history." I apologized for ruining that one model when I was little. He brushed his hand through my hair, told me not to worry about it. For a couple weeks there, sandwiched between cold silence and delirium, there was more than high-fives. But in the aftermath, I had forgotten, like a dream.

It was getting late. The bag of weed was empty, and we sat lifeless on my carpet, leaning against the foot of the sofa.

"So Murphy, I've been thinking. I think I know a way to help speed the process," she said.

"The process?"

"You know, your recurring dream."

"How?"

"I think I should sleep over tonight. I think sleeping in close proximity to someone with strong energies could focus your efforts. I'd be like the crystals, only stronger, because of all the posi   STURTEVANT dy."

"You're afraid of sleeping alone, aren't you. You think you'll have scary Exorcist nightmares."

"Yes. Shut up."

Soon after, we both fell exhausted onto my bed and slept.

I woke up in the early morning. The sun was just coming up and coloring my apartment a deep orange I had never seen before. Antoinette was buried under her dreadlocks, fast asleep on the other side of the bed. The pouch of crystals dangled from my neck. I grabbed the pad from my bedside table and went to the living room to write.

In the dream I saw my father, but he was healthy, and I wasn't screaming. I wasn't aware that he had died. He was wearing a brown monk's robe and was giving me a tour of the monastery where he now lived. It was a complicated house of many long rooms and secret corridors. He showed me all around the building, where he slept and where he studied everyday, where he sang in the choir. He thanked me for coming, and sadly said how I was the only one who had returned his calls. I was the only one who would see him, he told me.

Monastery: To be in a monastery in your dream suggests that you feel the need to do penance for some wrongdoing.

When I got out of the shower, Antoinette was up and making tea in the kitchen. My dream journal was on the coffee table. Racing past her in a towel, I grabbed it and retreated to my room to get dressed. She had made the bed.

"Good morning," she said when I came out.

"Good morning. Sleep well?"

"Like a baby. No nightmares. You?" She kept her eyes down on the mugs as she poured. I wondered if she had read it while I was in the shower, if she was just toying with me. She carefully walked over and bowed, serving the tea with an exaggerated smile.

"No nightmares," I said.

"Well, that's good. We're making progress."

We sat silently on the couch and cradled our steaming mugs under our chins, breathing in the aroma, waiting for it to cool. The room was different then, with her in it, the room lit up with daylight and both of us sober. It seemed bigger and somehow cleaner. I delicately sipped the tea and again had the feeling that she was right, that there is a right way and a wrong way to make a cup of tea, and that maybe, if I tried, I could accept that. It seemed perfectly plausible in it's own way, nothing supernatural about it. The whole thing looked differently now, the dream book, the crystals, the candlelit talks. It all seemed as distant and imaginary as the energies of Saturn. She hadn't read the journal, I was sure. If she felt anything like me, she was tired of dream analysis and spiritual growth. Those things of the night were different from the things of the morning. Maybe that's the reason dreams are so easy to forget.

"So why are you trying so hard to fly, anyway? What does flying mean?"

"Duh! Freedom!" she said, and laughed. It was all pretend. Nothing mattered anymore.

She went home to get ready for work. We were both due at the coffee shop in an hour. I brushed my teeth and fetched my wallet and keys from the table. The necklace of crystals was not on the bureau where I'd left it. I looked around the room and under the bed. She had taken it. One of the possible reasons dawned on me. I quickly opened my journal and looked over the entry I had written that morning. At the bottom of the page she had drawn a happy face. I flipped back to the earlier entry, about her and the jasmine tea and the kiss. At the bottom of that page, she had written, "In your dreams."

PETER MLADINIC

PRIVILEGE

You know how it is when you're 14
and 10 yr olds are hanging out.
We'd be down in the cellar gym
with the lime green shag rug and the mirrors,
benches and barbells, and every so often
they'd come in, the little kids, three of them
younger brothers, and we wouldn't hurt,
never hurt, but once in a while grab one
in a headlock and give him some knuckles
on the head, or bump, shove, trip.
That's how I remember him, one
of those kids. Anyway, he grew up
and became fairly rich. I'd venture to say
today he's worth over a million.
And what did he have? How did he
get that way? Never went to college,
never left home. Two older brothers,
the eldest a flunky, the other dead
at age 20, a drug overdose.
And the father always kept a German shepherd
chained in the back yard, and when
the dog got out and eventually was found,
or returned of its own volition, the father
would beat the dog, beat it sometimes
for the hell of it, to vent the bad
weather of a bad mood, so you'd
wonder about the people in that house,
the house the little kid grew up in.
Never went to college, struggled
to get through high school, but he worked
and bought and bought. Today
he owns a lot. And what did he have?
In the right place, at the right time.
Besides a work ethic and presumably
a head for business, he was white.
He had his race, his white skin.

So when someone says race is important
I think of him. He basically
had nothing, he beat the odds.
Had he been someone else,
in another skin, it might never have happened.
Also today, besides owning half the town,
he and his wife have two autistic children,
that to deal with. So even with millions
and his race, his own man, in his own skin,
there's a river to cross, a hill to climb,
steeper than those steps he took to and from
the cellar gym with its mirrors and barbells
and shag rug someone like me wrestled him to,
one of those kids who'd wonder what we were doing
down there, safe from the chained dog,
the flunkies and ones who'd keep them that way.

LIANNE SPIDEL

THE COMMON STONES HE SAVED

Home from the hunt at supper time
he would open his hand, each line
etched in sweaty grime, to reveal
a point unearthed by the plow, tip
intact, the color of sand, sunset
or obsidian. He always wondered

who had touched it last, before
it felled an animal or was lost
in the ransacking of a village,
then the stab of epiphany
measuring the time—2000 years—
against his own eleven.

In winter he turned to the common
stones he'd saved, plugged in
the rock tumbler, exchanging rough
grit for finer, washing between,
loving the feel of polish over form,
the first sight of true color.

Spring again, the hunt for fossils
disgorged in the rush of creeks:
cephalopod, horn coral, the rare
trilobite, little triune god,
its symmetry of bound segments
unmarred by 400 million years.

He was nearly grown when we left
behind the hills of limestone
and shale, oceanless tides deep
and still within them. After that
transilent time, any stone
he saw seemed just a common one.

LUCIA P. MAY

SUFFERING IS SUFFERING

After the morning session of War Poetry class
I sat in the cafe eating lunch, still shaking.
I just had an argument with a fellow student
who was a Vietnam vet.
He thought that a poem we were studying
about a Palestinian victim was politically
inflammatory because the poet was Palestinian.
Better not to erect walls for the reader, he said.
I said, *suffering is suffering*.
We glared at each other. I wanted to say,
Hey man, I married a Jew, have you?

As I ate lunch this fellow student
tripped at a stairway foundation by my table.
He fell face first. There were bloody scrapes
from a collision with the corner of my table
and food scattered on the floor.
Reflexively I sprang up to help him.
We didn't meet each others' eyes
when I offered him my sandwich
and knew he would have done so for me.

RACIST IN TRAINING, 1967

I'm seven. My parents and I
are in a Polish tour bus
going to Oswiecim.
The English way to say
it is Auschwitz.
The tourists on the bus eat
gooseberries and sing
Polish songs and prayers.
My father takes pictures.
Sometimes my mother smiles
with me for the pictures.
We ride past strawberry fields.
I love to crush ripe strawberries
on my cousins' bare backs when
they work in the fields.

My mother may still be mad
about Warsaw. In the hotel room
I turned on the radio full blast
and pretended to play a guitar.
When my father rushed in to make me
turn it down, I jumped on the bed
and shouted, *nigger music!*
My father flew at me and slapped
me hard in the face. *Don't ever
say that word again.* My ears were hot
and I thought I would burst.
He was always complaining
about nigger music.

My mother isn't smiling
when we arrive at the camp.
I'd apologize if I knew
she were mad at me.
No one looks at me.
There were wooden chairs
with arms but no seats. We see
rugs made from peoples' hair.

It doesn't hurt to get your hair cut.
There was a ton of it in that room.

My mother won't smile at me.
I want to tell her that we are Catholics
and could never be in this kind of trouble.
These people were Jews.
We're Americans, even Dad now.
The guides here say that the Nazis
were the meanest people in the world,
but my Uncle Edek said that
the Russians were the real pigs.
My grandfather said that Hitler
should have killed more Jews.

We go to a room
with two small box cars
on tracks that stop
at two oven doors in a brick wall.
This doesn't make sense.
How could they keep people
in these cars and dump them in an oven?
The people would just jump out.
Someone talks about how the showers
were another way to kill
people. Did they burn them
with hot water?

We leave the building
and this Polish lady runs out,
makes the sign of the cross
with one hand, squeezes
her babushka at her neck
with the other hand and cries,
Matko Boska, Matko Boska,
Mother of God.

MARTIN ELWELL

MY SISTER'S POEMS

Amnesia

I'm blonde today.   No one noticed.
So I lingered
outside an office,

waited for sweet-smelling women
to walk by in suits, pretended
I was one of them.   Security

guards escorted me
to the subway and left bruises
on my arm.   I enjoyed the attention.

I don't know who I am.
I wait in line with filthy men
for my dinner.

I avoid eye contact, always
staring at my plate.   I can't talk
to my family.   I thought

I recognized my brother
on the street yesterday, but I couldn't
speak.   He kept walking.

I didn't catch his eye.
I looked regretfully
into yellow living room windows

last night.   I remembered
calling him "Bud," watching
America's Funniest Videos

and laughing. Everyone's
a stranger now. Everyone
judges me. That's why I obsess

over eye liner, bite my nails,
smoke Marlboro Lights, and drink
whisky until I vomit. That's why

I sleep in parking garages
and unlocked cars. That's why
I dream of being home again.

BUTTERED POPCORN

I Google my sister's name about once a month now,

usually when I sit down with a bowl of popcorn

to watch TV.   I remember when the carpet was shag blue

and we watched syndicated episodes of the Brady Bunch together.

As Bobby and Cindy accused each other of stealing,

she lay back on the twin bed, her head propped up by pillows.

We ate buttered popcorn from an aluminum mixing bowl.

When Cindy's new trophy drove Bobby to jealously

enter an ice-cream-eating contest, we laughed.

We avoided the grayness of March.   Bobby and Cindy,

brother and sister, but not by blood, were lost

in the Grand Canyon.   I was twenty, but remembered laughing

with her twelve years earlier.   I haven't seen her since that day.

I went out with friends, and she left while no one was home.

I found her note folded neatly into a square on the coffee table.

I wondered if it was a suicide note, and I looked for her body

in the basement, bathrooms, bedrooms.   I didn't find her.

Ten years later, at thirty, I watched as Bobby and Cindy were rescued

before nightfall.   Everything worked out for the Bradys in the end.

I turned off the television and carried the bowl to the sink.

The unpopped kernels scratched and swished in salt.

MY ALUMINUM BASEBALL BAT

I never actually hit anyone with it,
but I was great at puffing out my chest
and cocking the bat, or leaning on it
as if to say, "I know you see my bat,
and I know you know I'll use it."
I was thirteen, and I didn't think
that anyone noticed my trembling hands.

The first time I might have brandished it,
our neighbor, Tom, was yelling at my mother.
She had made a comment about his drinking
and yelling at night with the windows open.
Tom pointed a finger at my mother's face,
but she stood firmly in the doorway, and I stood
firmly behind her, one hand clutching my bat.

The true test came later that summer.
My sister's boyfriend
shouted at her through the screen door
as his friends waited in the car.
Once again, I rushed to my room for the bat,
tucked in a bag under my glove.
I sweated with the anticipation

of busting into the street, maybe breaking
a windshield to send them peeling away.
When I came downstairs, he was crouching
beside her car, jabbing its tires with a knife.
I stopped stiff in the doorway, watching him
finish and drive away laughing.   Later,
my sister hugged me as I cried.

HOUSE ARREST

I obsessed over the lives of teenagers
on Beverly Hills 90210.   I envied

their resistance to cigarettes and rum drinks.
I kept spatulas and sauce pans

under my bed.   I found a boyfriend.
Despite his speed addiction and the gun shots

in his neighborhood, I moved in.
I became a morning regular at the liquor store.

First, I drank to calm my nerves before a test,
then for no reason.   I blacked out

weekly.   One morning, I woke up blonde
and laughed.   He kicked me out.

I hid my addiction and moved back home.
I kept bottles under my bed.

I thought no one would notice the missing
red wine or empty Budweiser cans.

I blacked out daily.   I lit my car on fire.
I hated the screeching noise it made.

I lit a friend's apartment building on fire
because I couldn't afford to pay the rent.

To avoid jail time, I took advantage of family-
connections and pity.

I embraced probation.   Why wouldn't I
violate it?   I already felt like a prisoner.

SNIPES

20 Marlboros / smoked in restaurant bathrooms / and private alleyways /
quarters quietly taken from mom's purse / and slid secretly / into the machine/

the pack found by my father / resulting in his lecture / and my sister's lies /
thrown into the trash / without a back-up plan / leaving an unsatisfied craving/

3 Marlboros / stolen from Uncle Paul's pack / one at a time /
her sideways exhale / through a cracked window / she was willing /

to risk discovery / determined to defy / and maturing her contempt /
she anticipated shouting matches / and punishments / the tensions of silence/

1 Marlboro / already half smoked / picked carefully from an ash tray /
a bent cigarette / stale and used / to satisfy her teenage addiction /

she was ashtray hunting / anything for a drag / searching the ground /
for a snipe / twisted into pavement / the taste of a stranger's spit /

MY SISTER'S FACE

Turning away from a homeless woman
sleeping on Boston Common was turning away
from my sister's violent hangover as I watched
her son play in the back yard.

Or pouring washer fluid into the well of my car
with the same precision she used to pour water
into our father's whiskey bottle, bringing
it level with the line he'd drawn on the label

after her first relapse.   Dunking my head
in the ocean resembled the time she jumped
into our pool to hide her intoxication after driving
with her three-year-old in the back seat.

I pretend to disown her in these memories,
just like she pretended to throw me a baseball,
faking over and over until she finally hit my nose,
sending me bloodied and crying into the house.

DIANE LEFER

CALIFORNIA ASPARAGUS

It's interesting how people treat a child who has killed.

All those years ago, my counselors never addressed the enormity of what I'd done, except to help me deal with the guilt. Well, of course there was guilt though it was an accident. I never meant to hurt Merry. It wasn't sibling rivalry. Even the word sibling is all wrong. My sister. My sister Meredith, Merry, that's the sound of relationship, of two little girls at home alone. I was eleven. She was five. Sibling is so clinical. It robs her of even more than the life I took from her.

Afterwards, when I returned to school – a new school, a different school, a place I only lasted a few weeks – it didn't matter. Everyone still knew. The kids stared at me and then avoided me till a fat girl asked, "What does it feel like?" I didn't answer. "I heard you killed your sister."

"I did not," I said.

I liked the fat girl. No one else spoke to me. "What does it feel like," I said, "to be such a fat freak?"

I'm a nicer person since I married Rudy. We are both tall and thin. Our daughter Kira stands in the last row of her fifth-grade class photograph. A year from now, she'll be the same age I was when it happened, and a few years younger than Javi who hasn't yet killed anyone as far as I know but tried to. "I had to," he told me. "He shot my dog."

"Why would anyone shoot a dog?" I said, shocked, before I remembered that dog means homeboy.

Kira goes to a safe suburban school and most likely will never kill anyone or witness a person getting killed. The trouble she'll get into will grow from normal adolescence and from boredom.

Just this year she stopped calling me Mommy and began to call me Mom. To my mother, I'm still Cathy. Merry, trailing after me, used to call Cath-E-E-E-E! As a teenager, I changed it to Callie—my secret reference to Kali, Goddess of death and destruction who some (at least in India) consider beautiful. In Guatemala they called me Cati and that's what Rudy calls me. And Tony. At the office they call me Catherine. No one has ever called me Kate. Some friends call me Cath. Javi calls me Miss.

I visit him in the Burn Center where they transferred him after Rudy stabilized him in the ER. The team will work toward his recovery until such time as the authorities decide what to do with him.

Javi. Javier. He refuses to use an English name or street name. "Javi. Because that's what my mother called me."

The first time, I went without wanting to and didn't see him. The medical plaza building loomed over the Burn Center like a chalk white cliff that I was supposed to scale without a rope. I had to tell myself it might be interesting. Instead of a lobby, I found a narrow hallway where the security guard scared me off with "What are you looking for, Ma'am?" a challenge rather than "Can I help you?" an offer.

Javi didn't go directly to the Burn Center. Rudy saw him first. Got him on IV liquids, cut through the chest wall because the kid couldn't breathe.

"He's got no one," Rudy said. That's all he told me–confidentiality. Just: "Visit him. Just sit and listen." But it's easy to say no to a husband. There's a give and take. The man you're married to can only push so hard.

"No," I said.

So Rudy got Tony to ask.

"No," I said. By then I knew more. The TV news didn't use Javi's name but they gave the story plenty of play. "I burned a house down. He burned a house. That doesn't make us the same."

"Cati–"

"He didn't just set the fire. He tried to shoot the people when they ran out."

"You're talking about a child." Tony chants, a Buddhist, which perhaps accounts for his overabundance of compassion. I too used to chant whenever I heard a siren: Heart attack, not fire, heart attack, not fire.... "Neighborhoods like his are a war zone," Tony said. "He's a child."

When you stay friends with a former lover, you tend to make an effort, you want to think well of each other. And so when Tony asked and asked again, I said yes.

Then down one hall and another to Javi's room. They made me wear a mask and also gloves though I was told I must not touch him.

The doctors won't allow him to be handcuffed to the bed, so there's a young cop stationed at the door. He wants my ID. He wants to know my relationship.

"My husband treated him in the ER," I say.

"What for?" the cop asks.

"For his injuries."

"No. I mean what for?"

The odor in his room: like the smelly stuff they once put on me, that ointment and something musty covered by something sickly sweet covered by something antiseptic with another sweet smell on top of it failing to disguise the pungent which fails to disguise the smell of rot.

How do you overcome the gag reflex? What do you do with a gangbanger who is doped against the pain and covered with bandages and has a tube in his throat so he can't speak? Is he even going to live? He's got a breathing tube, a feeding tube, so many machines glowing. Where his skin remains exposed, something oozes, but whether it's salve or his own body fluids, I don't know. There's a burbling, aquarium sound and a scritch scritch sound like a cat in the litter box, scratching against sand. His elbows rest on the bed, his hands big and white with bandages, a cartoon character's hands, raised as if in blessing in the air. He hears you enter and his eyes open a minute outlined in bandages, one eye big and round, the other rolled back leaving the reddened white visible only as a slit, and how do you feel during that fraction of an instant before these eyes close and you see expectation and what looks so briefly like hope?

"I set a fire, too." What a stupid thing to say. "I was only in the hospital a day or two."

Or so I've been told. I don't remember being there, but I do remember the smell of smoke and singed hair that never seemed to leave me till the day I suddenly noticed it was gone, and I remember the pain that tore through me when I breathed, worse when I sobbed, a fire raging in my raw windpipe and throat. I knew I deserved the pain. I never tried to stop the sobs, but once the body's repression kicked in, they stopped on their own and I found myself unable to cry.

"You'll have to step outside," said the nurse.

"Well," I said, "I've got to go. Pick up my daughter at school."

Javi agitated a bandaged hand, each finger wrapped in gauze, like five white sausages or worms. I held the alphabet board and he pointed out the letters: V I S I T.

Oh shit.

His eyes stayed open. P L E A S --

Andrea, who wants to be called Drea, is not someone I would call a friend. Our relationship is about conserving fossil fuels and so we drive in her Land Rover to pick our daughters up from school and we wait, engine running, wasting, polluting, doing what the Catholic Church has just pronounced a sin, but at least we've carpooled. In Guatemala, morning and afternoon the cars lined up, too, in front of the school I attended but with chauffeurs and bodyguards waiting, not soccer moms. I've told her this before and so, as she often does, Drea regards the line and says, "Not quite Guatemala."

Guatemala is where I was sent after changing schools twice didn't help. My parents sent me to live for a year with an old friend of my mother's who had married a man named César Mondragón. The Mondragóns had a daughter my age who attended a boarding school in New Rochelle, New York. "I don't see why we don't swap," Mrs. Mondragón said, and then asked me to call her Tía. "Margot could live with your parents while you live here." She obviously had no idea what was going on. By the time I returned to the United States, my parents had sold our house, moved, separated, and were waiting for the divorce to be final.

Now I'm a suburban Mom. Here we have harmony in diversity, where the Priuses line up with the Hummers. I wear an orange silicone bracelet that reads IMPEACH BUSH and CHENEY. My daughter wears a thick purple rubber band from the crisper drawer: CALIFORNIA ASPARAGUS. Drea thinks the personal is political while I've begun to think the reverse.

She says, "In principle, I'm all for universal health care, but why should I pay taxes to take care of people who won't take responsibility for themselves? Look at those girls over there. They're fat."

Interesting. I say it's interesting how people treat a child...like me. You were responsible for her death, said one of the counselors. You didn't kill her. What sort of distinction is that? What sort of word is interesting and what sort of person would choose it?--so objective as to be abnormal, so let me explain I often try to look at what happened as if it had occurred to someone else. There's the idea that if I look at this guilty little girl from a distance, I might feel compassion.

And it's interesting that the mostly unspeakable event that led to so much disruption and pain, this thing that one of my counselors assured me was part of my past but did not define me as a person, became the hallmark of my identity as soon as I discovered sex. By the time I was 28, I'd had three proposals of marriage from men who wanted to save me or maybe punish me and who were careful to say, "Of course we'll never have children."

And this part of my past changed my career path. After one year of law school I quit, worried I'd never pass the good character test you need to be admitted to the Bar. My juvenile record is sealed but I've hardly kept it a secret. And as to moral character, not only did I kill my sister, but for years I used that fact to pick up men. I told myself they should know the worst thing about me before we got started but the truth is I believed it made me more interesting, seductive. What kind of morality is that?

So I scaled back my ambitions. I'm a legal assistant, doing deposition summaries and digests which turns out to be convenient as I can work most days from home. I prefer not to know which side my firm is on. Then I can do a good job without bias. So when the EMT says "I arrived on the scene and it was dark and first thing, I said was, Get some lights over here, I can't see," someone other than me decides whether to use the words I've highlighted or try to suppress them so that the jury can decide what constitutes reasonable responsibility.

And because I wanted children, I began to seek out foreign men, men who came from violent places where it was nothing unusual to lose a child to war or accident or preventable disease. Rudy and I clicked. We had Guatemala in common. We married on April 22, 1996. We had our daughter Kira.

I don't tell my story anymore, but I still dream about my sister.

Merry is wearing a beauty pageant tiara and then she is fucking my husband. Not Rudy, another husband who doesn't exist.

She is trying to protect Kitty from the attack of huge grasshoppers and while my feet are frozen to the ground, Merry is covered in a swarm of wings.

We are on the swings in the playground but we are all grown, adult and we swing higher and higher until she flies out into space and I wake up screaming. My screams wake Kira who wakes up screaming and in this way, the pain is passed on and my husband doesn't know which one of us to calm first and my daughter fears something she doesn't know and cannot name.

What on earth made each of us relocate here? Southern California, where every year hills and houses burn and I have to smell smoke in the air and see ash fallen on our patio like snow, where I sit transfixed by round-the-clock coverage of wildfires and quickly kill the picture if Rudy or Kira walks into the room, like someone hiding internet porn; where Javi's mother brought him, still a baby; where Rudy with his Spanish name and accent is mistaken for uneducated, low class and must be reminded without respite of violence.

Rudy: His thin face, his glasses, the thin golden metal frames that I think would suit an old school Irish priest. Rudy is eleven years my senior and seems even older. Meeting him socially you wouldn't guess that he's a surgeon. A gold tooth – Third World dentistry, not bling. The dark suits that hang on his frame when he's not in surgical gown. Awkward. I looked at him and knew I could have him and the security of being a doctor's wife. Not the money, but the idea that he was good at saving children, a guarantee, I thought, that our children would not die.

Rudy saves kids all the time. He says he went into emergency medicine because of the regular shifts, the chance to have a regular family life but I think he likes it, working in the 'hood, witness to so much trauma. And I like it that Rudy looks inside a person only in the most literal way, his hands deep inside the body's wounds. Still it's difficult when he comes home angry, depressed, refusing to eat or speak. He's coiled, tense.

Sometimes it's worse when the blood and trauma energize him, his eyes glittery, his speech fast and broken by laughter. When death invigorates him. Sometimes he works on a kid with old bullet wounds and I ask doesn't he wonder whether he worked on this same kid before? They blend into each other, though some are gangbangers, some innocent kids caught in the crossfire. Some live and some do not. To Rudy, they are wounds, hearts, brains, lungs, spinal cords. And they are children. Some are killers and he tries to save them. He patches them up, then sends them–where? Off to Juvenile Hall or prison or back to the streets.

At parties, when people challenge him, he starts to make excuses for these kids and then looks to me, as though my situation is the same and I can explain it and help him. When I stay silent, he shrugs.

"A surgeon's nothing but a mechanic," he says. "A mechanic repairs your car. It's not his responsibility how you drive."

I don't know what made him care so much for Javi.

Whose eyes I can just glimpse, open behind the white bandages, when I tell him the story I used to tell so often. The men used to say You seem so comfortable with yourself, with what happened. Were they impressed? Appalled? Even Rudy who guards his privacy who s   Lefer   1 to deal with, who doesn't want to burden me or Kira w... ., ... are things he would rather not remember to which I reply, What good is rather not when I'm sure you do?, even Rudy was attracted to me because of the way you tell your story, as if you're comfortable with it.

It's just words, like the way men used to smile at how I said fuck without it sounding angry or dirty.

So: In the house where I grew up, which was not here in Southern California, there was an electric heater in the bathroom. Mr. Heater-Upper, Eater-Upper. We loved the red glow, my little sister Merry and I, and the smell that came off the electric coils. And one winter day, I had the bright idea to hold our scarves and sweatshirts and jackets and gloves against the grill to get them toasty warm. A lick of flame came tongueing out. I dropped the clothes. Flames leaped. The toilet paper caught, the shower curtains smouldered. I splashed water with the toothbrush cup but the flames spread and so did the fumes, carbon monoxide and what I eventually learned was hydrogen cyanide from the plastic curtains and the woolen scarves. I was eleven years old, running blinded by smoke, squirming on the floor as I reached under the couch to Kitty's hiding place.   Staying low to the ground may be what saved me. As for Merry, I suppose I could claim I imagined she'd flown out the window on fairy wings or escaped to the secret world we called The Children's Land. In truth, I forgot all about her. I just forgot. I held tight to the cat and I ran.

I don't remember being in the hospital. "I wasn't there very long, not like you, Javi." I had smoke inhalation and minor burns, but from what I've been told they were mostly concerned about the possibility of infection, especially where they painted smelly stuff on my little girl's flat chest, there where the skin was breached, where the terrified cat had clung to me, digging deep with her claws. "When you get hurt, you find out who your friends are," Javi says.
"You mean your dogs?" I say. "They won't see you long as there's a cop at the door."
"Miss," he says. "You said dogs!"
In places where the gauze has been removed, his skin is white and waxy and in places red and ropy, not his real color at all. There's some kind of stuff where the cartilage should be on his ears and what's left of his nose. He can't have a pillow–too much pressure. And the nurse comes in and draws the curtain around him to empty his bag or change the dressings or do whatever a nurse does in private.

One day Drea told me a story that made me understand why those men didn't trust me with children. In the town where she grew up there was a woman who had two children and when they were two and four years old, she drowned them. Not guilty by reason of insanity, she spent years in the State hospital. Then came the era when the hospitals were all shut down and Reagan cut the funds and mental patients ended up on the streets. Not this woman. She married one of her doctors. They lived in the house next door to Drea. She was very beautiful and friendly. She liked to sing "Paper Moon." She and the doctor had two children. She was a doting mother. When the children were two and four, she drowned them.
The night after Drea tells me this story, I wake in a panic. I can't swallow, I can't breathe. Slowly, gradually, I calm down listening to Kitty purr beside me till I remember where I am in the quiet night, alone, there is no cat, Rudy's at the hospital, my daughter sleeping peacefully (I hope) in her own bed and the night so quiet I can hear the refrigerator all the way from the kitchen, humming like a warm pet.
It must have been that story that got me thinking about Reagan. I sit at the computer reading about him. It's interesting that the same man responsible for turning so many people out onto the street also started the corporate incarceration industry to lock people up. It looks like privatization started right there, channeling funds to companies to round up the Haitians and Marielitos and put them behind barbed wire when they reached our shores fleeing for their lives. And in Guatemala? Tony says, "Well, of course there were targeted assassinations, but the massacres of whole villages? That didn't start with

impunity till Reagan."

Reagan starts to enter my dreams along with Merry.

She is wearing denim and very big glasses. She says "The only Evil Empire was Reagan's own." In the dream, I start to shiver, cold as ice. "His conspiracy with transnational capital," says Merry.

Then I dream she's going down on him while I shout No! No! No! I know I'm dreaming and I tell myself this is what girls always do. We dream about powerful men. But what did my baby sister know of politics or cocks? Nothing. Nothing. Nothing. The woman in the dream is all grown up. How did I know it was Merry? In a dream you just know. What did she look like? She looked like me.

I must look suspicious because it looks like the nurse is suspicious of me.

"Wait outside," she says.

I'm not a social worker or a lawyer. What am I? A middle class underemployed suburban doctor's wife. And so she must wonder. What the hell am I doing with this boy? Damned if I know.

"If you're entertaining notions about sexual healing..."

Did she really say that? The truth is, I want to put my arms around him and hug him, but in his condition, it would hurt, and anyway, I can see it's not allowed. Sexual healing? Isn't that a song? I think, but I don't say it. And I don't tell her this boy and I have a lot in common.

It's interesting the way they build houses in Southern California as if they can't admit it ever gets cold. I do not allow space heaters. Rudy and Kira are gone most of the day so they don't mind, but in the winter, sometimes I give up trying to get any work done. Just try clicking the mouse and typing with your gloves on.

And it's interesting that Rudy and I connected because we had Guatemala in common even though neither one of us has ever wanted to or thought of going back. For me, that year is part of my life, part of who I am, just like the fire and not something I would have chosen.

It seemed a somber city of somber people but the real problem was I didn't want to be there. People asked "What are you doing here?" and I would say "Learning Spanish," though we only spoke English in the Mondragón home and I went to an English-language school. When the local girls gossiped in Spanish, I didn't always understand and was just relieved I never overheard César Mondragón's name. Hanne, diplomat's daughter from Denmark, spoke English with such a heavy accent, I wasn't always sure I got it: that Lupe's father was the chief of police, Angela's father a drugs boss. We wore uniforms but there were no rules about what we wore beneath. The more developed girls showed off their US-manufactured underwear, with much prestige accruing to those who wore a Maidenform bra. I was too young and flat to need one. When would my breasts grow? Would the scars from Kitty's claws ever fade? There were always flowers. There were always mountains. There was always steak for breakfast and the sweetest oranges in the world. There were servants. I didn't even have to make my bed, but I felt like a prisoner. I was never allowed out alone. My classmate Carmen had once been kidnapped and held for ransom. Don Miguel, the chauffeur, drove me to and from class. Once he showed me his gun. "Of course," said Tía. "A chauffeur is also a bodyguard." I was afraid of kidnappers, but curious. Anyway, I was a killer. Would they dare? I tagged along in department stores when Tía shopped for Lladró porcelains–true art, I thought, the epitome of graceful beauty. By marrying a foreigner, she'd got herself a huge house, and Ana the cook, and Eugenia the maid--a Jehovah's Witness who lived on the roof with her painfully thin daughter, and a bodyguard-chauffeur, and money to buy all the porcelain figurines she wanted while, even before the fire, my parents argued, my mother crying "Where do you want me to economize? I even cut my own hair." And I remember crying in the winter from the cold and how Mom sighed and said "Put on another sweater" and how every time I went into the bathroom I counted on Mr. Heater-Upper Eater-Upper to warm me.

During these shopping trips in Guatemala, I would try to separate myself from Tía. Sometimes, when Don Manuel stopped the car at a light near an ice cream cart, I'd jump out and run off pretending I just had to buy some. How could people tell I was American? Whenever I managed to be alone, someone would approach. They'd walk close by without looking me in the face. There would be whispers. When you go home, tell the Americans this government tortures. The police chief is a killer. Once a very thin woman with penciled-in thin eyebrows passed me a note. A ransom note, I thought, but when I unfolded the little piece of paper in my room I read, No somos libres. We are not free.

Here's a Guatemala story I heard from Tony.

This guy Eduardo had gambling debts and so he needed to sell his car. He went for a test drive with a prospective buyer. He didn't know the man was a union leader. They were ambushed by a death squad, the car sprayed with machine gun fire. The union leader was killed and Eduardo critically injured. Someone called an ambulance which transported the two bodies to the hospital where an orderly recognized the union leader which meant this was not a robbery gone bad but a political killing and so no one dared treat Eduardo. They let him bleed out in the entry. No one told Rudy, who'd gone to college prep with both

Eduardo and Tony and was working in the ER just steps away.

They didn't tell Rudy because he'd spent too much time in Mexico. They were afraid he'd forgotten that a person must be careful.

Much of what I know about my husband's life in Guatemala I know from Tony, that Rudy got his medical degree in Mexico which meant that after he graduated, he owed national service to that country. He was assigned to work in a Triqui village. His having saved the lives of Indians–even though, truth be told, he still had the prejudices of his class and didn't very much like them--when he returned home to Guatemala he was suspect. There were death threats. Firebombs. That's how he ended up in California.

And this is the advantage of being an American. Rudy treats anyone who comes in the door. Aside from that, it must seem as though nothing has changed. Still the bullet-riddled bodies, the stupid bloody allegiances, but at least here, the dead have all their fingers, their genitals have not been sliced off and stuffed into their mouths, their bones aren't broken, and only rarely are the bodies burned.

And I'm with Drea as we wait in a line of MiniCoopers and Priuses and SUV's, engines running. These children are picked up by mothers and nannies not, as far as I can tell, by bodyguards with guns, but the engines just the same are running.

"Why are you so mad at Reagan?" she says. "What about Bush?" But everyone knows Bush is a criminal. It's scary how we romanticize Reagan. Drea's mad about the war and the economy and the way the feds don't respect California's medical marijuana law.

She's telling me why drugs should be legal but when the kids climb in, she turns her head to the backseat. "Not," she says, "for children."

"Tío Antonio!" Kira throws her arms around Tony. "¿Qué pasa?, calabaza." These days when I touch her, just to smooth her hair, she pulls away. Kira won't talk Spanish to her father. She makes fun of his accent and I think she finds it embarrassing, but to Tony it's always "Tío, ¿qui'ubo?"

I was more or less in love with Tony until the day (or night) he followed his heart (or dick) and chose to live his life in the US as a gay man. (Yes, I got tested.) It was Tony who introduced me to my husband. I liked the fact that Tony's coming out didn't faze Rudy a bit. They continue to hug each other when they meet and when they part though I suppose for them an abrazo is as formal as a handshake.

"Tío Antonio!" When Kira was a baby, Tony would toss her in the air and catch her to my horror and her delight. Rudy would never have done such a thing. He's the father who fastened her so carefully into the car seat. Who always held her hand gently and firmly and made her look both ways even after the light turned green. I found it was too easy to lose her, she was so quick and small, I'd say a word to an adult or look up at the sky and just like that, in an instant, Kira would be gone. When she was with Rudy, he never lost track. Tonight he's on the four-to-midnight.

I take the pizza from Tony and he hoists Kira in his arms and swings her.

"She's getting too big for that," I say.

"Don't molest the wildlife!" she shrieks. I'm not sure where she got that.

Not that there's anything, to use the word, inappropriate about Tony. When Kira was smaller, he demonstrated the "side hug" in which he squatted beside her and let her put her arms around him while he turned away. This was the only contact permitted, the principal had told him, between him and his second graders, and we'd laughed, how ridiculous! Rudy of course touches people's bodies all the time. It's his job. Tony once thought giving warm abrazos to children was part of his job as well.

"No le hace," says Tony and after one more swing deposits her lightly on her feet.

He's short, but solid. I know she doesn't really weigh too much for him. I know his strength because there was a time when he had no trouble lifting and carrying me.

Pizza night, informal, we eat at the kitchen island. No pepperoni. Kira is a vegetarian these days. She serves the chilled asparagus she made with lemon vinaigrette and asks, "¿Dónde está Jack?"

"Union meeting."

Lately, Jack always seems to be somewhere, something else I don't mention.

Tony and Jack advocate monogamy in principle but balk at strict adherence.

Tía told me Latin men all cheat. This is something Rudy and I have never discussed. But I think so do Anglo men. Asian men. Men. Not to mention women.

Tía said before she married César Mondragón he had to sign everything over, put everything he owned in the world in her name.

"Ah, you gringos," says Tony. "Sounds just like the IMF."

Then he starts in about Argentina: "The economic miracle of Latin America till the Generals went for Chicago economics and plunged the middle class – more than half the population – into poverty. God bless America," he says.

"I don't believe in God anymore," Kira says. "God lets people eat animals."

"That's not all he allows," I say.

"That's why I don't eat meat. I don't allow it for me!"

It must be childhood innocence that makes animals worth as much as people, that makes us responsible for animals even as people are left to look out for themselves.

"Have you been back to the Burn Center?" asks Tony.

I have been but this conversation is not appropriate in front of my daughter.

"What's the matter? She's seen worse on CSI."

"And I wish she wouldn't."

He knows more about children than I do. I want to trust him and he's so goodnatured, in the end I always do. Then I remind myself that when we were going out how often he'd call at the last moment to cancel and sometimes wouldn't even bother to call. If he didn't show up, wasn't it clear he had canceled? And the time he and Jack took a three-day weekend. "That's why they have substitutes on call." He's so awfully good but only when he's being good.

"Is the tube out yet?"

I tell him they've had to do more cutting to save his arms. How with so much pain, Javi's finally getting the narcotics he wanted. How his whole respiratory apparatus is a holy mess.

"Is he talking?"

"Oh, yeah," I say. "I liked him better when he couldn't. He told me after he firebombed the building, it occurred to him there would be drugs stashed there. So the idiot runs inside to look instead of running away."

"That proves he's just a child," Tony says. "No impulse control."

"Pobre niño," says Kira. And I realize both she and I give Tony what we won't give Rudy.

"Would you say blacks are Anglos?" I ask Drea. "I mean is Anglo anyone who has English for a mother tongue?" She looks at me like I'm crazy. "You know. Jews, blacks, Irish, etc. Anglos?"

"What difference does it make?"

For a change I have to admit she's right.

Javi's bandages are off. Today they didn't make me wear a mask but I wish they had, to hide my shock. The sight of him penetrates me fast and then my eyes glaze over because I cannot bear to see him. The narrow slit eye has a purple swollen lump above it coming out of his forehead like a Frankenstein bolt and the flesh below hangs in a melted bulbous mass. His neck and arms brown and purple and red. As if he wants to shock me more, he tells me about the first time he shot someone. Flat tone, no emotion, and I have to hold down my own emotion, the chill, and I tell myself he talks that way because it's physical, because of the way his mouth contracts into an awful scar-tissue sneer.

They will work on his arms and legs, skin grafts, stretching exercises and therapy so that he can regain function. But as for surgery on his face, that's cosmetic, not covered. The melted flesh will remain as is.

If our faces–laugh lines, wrinkles--tell the world who we are, Javi's face tells the world I am a monster.

"I'm not proud of what I did," he says, "but I did what I had to do."

His words don't sound rehearsed so much as automatic.

"Why?" I ask.

"You wouldn't get it," he says. "Law of the street."

I want to say You've been brainwashed but instead I ask, "Were you arrested?"

"No."

"You shouldn't talk about it then."

"So I'll go back to Juvie," he says.

I don't know if I'm trying to protect him or show him how little he knows: "They'll try you as an adult so fast, you won't know what hit you."

And I feel deflated and then I fill up again but it's with rage. I'm so mad at him, and at Rudy for patching kids up and sending them back to those streets where it will just happen again and again and for the insurance rules that will leave him with this face, and at Kira for being so fucking privileged she thinks it makes a difference that she won't eat meat and at Tony for talking me into being here and Margot, Tía's daughter, who didn't let me know when her mother was dying in a hospital in Miami and my mother and my father for never letting me know how much they blamed themselves, and rage and disappointment at myself because I can't handle this.

I can't stand that I told him about Merry and he didn't say anything unless you count, "You were eleven. When I was eleven, I had a Glock." He shoots people. He doesn't care. Not about me, not about anyone. Though can it be normal? That children are self-centered? Adolescents are narcissistic. Maybe it's that children don't yet have empathy. But I can remember Merry at the playground, when she put her hand on the slide right on top of a yellow jacket and it stung her. I was terrified of being stung but Merry was so little I told our mother I wished it had happened to me instead. Isn't that empathy? And when the war began, Kira cried for the Iraqi children.

My stomach starts to jump. I can't stand this kid. I get up to leave but his eyes fixed on me remind me of something and I stand there hoping I'll recognize what it could be.

Sometimes I think I love my husband the way I loved my cat– with a reciprocated fierce attachment and no idea what goes on inside him.

"Rudy doesn't trust me," I said once to Tony.

"You have to understand. We grew up with the idea that to survive, you have to watch what you say and who you say it to."

Then maybe he wouldn't have treated Eduardo, I think.

"But you're not like that," I say.

"Once my big secret was out, I let go of all."

"What are you doing?" I ask my husband. "Having your revenge on us gabachos by putting these kids back on the street?"

"Those kids," he says, "live in a war zone. What do you do with child soldiers? You've got to demobilize them. Heal them in body and mind. I do my part of it. It's not my fault if the rest of the job doesn't get done."

This sounds like the most honest answer he's given yet about his work.

And I remember when I was in high school how I watched as my classmates got into fights, got caught with drugs or knives, stole cars, burglarized the homes where they or their girlfriends babysat and if they weren't white, they got sent away, and if they were, their parents were asked to put them in private school.

"You can't just punish them," my husband says. "They need to be part of society. And they need a decent society to be part of."

And I realize it was Kitty's eyes I was trying to remember. She was such a good cat and I was an irresponsible child. It was my job to feed her and sometimes I forgot. I'd be teasing Merry or playing with my breakfast instead of eating it. Kitty wouldn't cry or meow or paw at my leg. But I'd suddenly be aware she was watching me. I'd meet those big round eyes and know she wanted not just food but something more. She wanted to but wasn't sure she could trust me.

I returned from Guatemala and Kitty was gone. The child I'd been was gone. A normal irresponsible child who made ordinary mistakes. Before I killed, the way I loved was clean and simple. I loved my cat and understood she hurt me only because she was terrified.

So you love and take care of your husband, you love and take care of your child, you help out your mother whether or not she was the world's greatest mother, you hold down a job, you wear an orange silicone bracelet, you believe yourself to be involved, concerned, productive and then you realize you've spent the last thirty years of your life all the time mostly thinking about yourself. Am I the one who lacks empathy?

It takes willpower to look at Javi, he is so hideous. Merry died of smoke inhalation. My parents at least had that: no disfigurement. Their little girl dead still looked like their little girl.

"You know what I keep thinking about," I say to Javi. "I'm trying to figure out, Can you have love without empathy?"

"Yes, Miss," he says instantly. "I can explain that to you. After what I been

through, I don't feel nothing for no one. But I love my mother."
And I look at him, at that face, without flinching and I ask him to tell me about her.

Javi tells me his father was killed. His mother survived the massacre with baby Javi in her arms. Somehow she got them to the United States. He doesn't remember much about his childhood. When he started school, a neighbor picked him up from kindergarten and he was supposed to stay with her until his mother got home from the sweatshop. The neighbor smelled funny and he didn't like her and she always made him kneel and pray.
"One day I did bad," he told me. "My Mom was always telling me to do good, but I got so mad at that lady, I kicked her."
When his mother came to get him, he was afraid he'd be punished. "The door opens and I'm outta there." His mother chased him and caught up to him under a streetlight. "She grab onto me and smack me. So I start screaming. She's all yelling and crying and whacking me and shouting Why, Javi, why? only in Spanish." Someone called the cops. "They take her on this child abuse charge and then they sent her back to Guatemala." He's been in and out of group homes and institutions ever since. "It's my fault," he says. "I wish I wouldn't've did that." He looks at me. Those eyes. "I can't blame nobody but me."

Demobilize them, says my husband. He says it's the same as war.
It's called a firefight when soldiers shoot at one another, though we don't dignify these kids with the name of soldiers and our opponents overseas are simply terrorists, even when they're 15 years old. Like Omar Khadr who I keep reading about on-line when I'm at the computer, supposedly working on a deposition.
His parents took him to Afghanistan to live under the Taliban. He was a well behaved, polite Muslim boy. When he was fifteen, US forces invaded and he fought back. The US dropped two 500-pound bombs on the house where he was staying with other fighters. He took two bullets in the back. He's been accused of throwing a grenade that killed an American soldier but isn't that what you do in war? He was taken from Afghanistan to Guantánamo. He's been there six years. He's gone through puberty and adolescence, most of it in solitary. Without books, without school, without being treated as human. He was short-shackled - i.e., his wrists shackled together and his ankles shackled together and then his wrists shackled to his ankles. He was placed in a painful position and left there for hours. When he called the guards because he had to use the bathroom, they wouldn't let him. When he peed on himself, they

poured a bucket of PineSol over him, then grabbed him and used his shackled body as a mop to swab the   floor.

So I'm telling this story to Drea and it's obvious she isn't interested and I think of an advice column in the paper that made Kira laugh: The greatest gift of friendship is to now and then listen patiently while your friend bores you. We wait for the children, our engine running.

"You can't blame him for how his parents raised him." There are international conventions, you know. And she does know. It's not that Drea is unaware. The woman listens to NPR. She agrees: Child soldiers are supposed to be demobilized and rehabilitated, not punished. All over the world, billions are being spent to reintegrate children into society. I've heard that in Afghanistan alone, the US has spent $2 million–but not for Omar Khadr. "I mean look at our kids," I say. "They're brainwashed by us. How can a child be held responsible?"

The girls open the door and climb in with the smell of car exhaust and star jasmine and my daughter is crying. "Mrs. Lewis says we have to kill Iraqis because they attacked us on 9/11." The woman is already suspect–a Mrs. rather than a Ms. "Mom," Kira says, "I know it's a lie." My daughter is sobbing and I can't reach her over the headrest of the front seat. Vanessa stares out the window. "Please don't go to school. Please don't complain. Please don't tell I told you." No death squads here, but it's still a good idea to keep your head down. "I know she's lying, but please don't do anything."

I just want to give Kira backup, the way a mother should.

Where were my parents–Merry's and mine? I don't remember. I don't remember watching the house burn. There must have been a funeral for Merry. Most likely I wasn't even there. There was a motel room we stayed in and then we stayed with Grandma, and there were different schools, and counselors, and the fat girl, and Guatemala.

When I returned, my parents were living apart.

"We found Kitty a good home," they said and in spite of my suspicions I chose to believe them.

Kira wants to know why we can't have space heaters like everyone else and one day, though I probably should not have, I finally told her why I'm afraid of fire. "Where was Grandma?" she asked.

Now of course my mother lives in a modest one-bedroom apt in North Hollywood and we pay the rent. But then? "I don't remember."

"Where was Grandpa?" I just don't know. "Your parents are supposed to take care of you," she said.

And I realized that whenever Rudy and I take a weekend together, we ask Tony to babysit, and not my mother.

"Do you know where your mother is?" I ask.

Javi shakes his head. His mother can't read or write. At first, she had people write for her. Her address changed. His address changed again and again.

I sent the Mondragons a letter or two after I left and for a few more years a Christmas card and then nothing.

He looks at me. Those eyes. Or rather that eye. One is still half-covered with melted flesh. I don't know if it's harder for him to see out of it or harder for me to look at it.

One day someone gives him a mirror.

He looks. He gulps hard. Then: "No one's gonna mess with me now," he says. "I like it." Every time I soften toward him, he says something that chills me to the soul. I can't quite hold it: The polite little child inside the would-be killer. The violent boy inside the sweet shy child.

I held the clothes against the heater with my own two hands. Javi kicked the lady in the shins and bit her hand like an animal which is how an animal speaks without words asking you to please just understand.

We know exactly what we've done and there's something very comforting about our guilt. Knowing our responsibility. It's clear as mud, my second-grade teacher used to say and I never understood that—a strange idiomatic phrase that I'm sure Tony never says to the second grade.

Javi's mouth is disfigured but I think he is smiling. And then he isn't.

"Miss," he says. "What's gonna happen to me?"

I don't know. I don't even know about asparagus. My daughter's rubber band reminds me how ignorant I am. I eat it. I know you can't pick it the year you plant it. What you get develops over time.

And the lawyers I work for can't answer my questions. They don't know much about immigration law but they figure even if his mother had applied for asylum, a child abuse charge would have ended her chances. And since we're not allowed to send a child into an abusive situation, he must have then become a ward of the state, complete with a green card they can now take away. And of course without his Mom, Javi's flat voice has told me of abuse and violence, neglect, and more abuse. Foster mothers, even the good ones, overwhelmed by even more than his own mother had to face, whole housefuls of troubled children, kids who did damage to one another, and the poverty, and the violence of the streets. "I got jumped in young," he says. "They had my back. I had my homies to protect me."

Perhaps the closest he'll come to saying he was scared.

"I got shot twice," he says. "I almost died tweaking. I stopped breathing. I was like a dead person that time but I don't want to die." Who is the boy inside this body? Where is the soul inside this boy? "If they send me back, that's OK," he says. "I'll find my mother."

"You don't know where she lives."

He says, "I know where to look. There's a Guatemala inside Guatemala."

The Guatemala inside Guatemala. It's in my head like a song you can't shake. The Guatemala of the Indians. Guatemala of the poor. Guatemala of the rich. Walls bristling with shards of broken glass. The highrises with armed guards on each floor. The artist who came to Tía's and painted a mural on the dining room wall, a panorama of dugout canoes on volcanic lakes, monkeys in the trees, Spanish convents, processions, a woman kneeling before a stone lighting candles, ruins in a jungle. César Mondragón explaining to me that's Panajachel, that's Tikal, he said the words as though he could taste their flavor, Antigua, Quiriguá. There–that's the pilgrimage to the Black Christ of Esquipulas. You see the carpet of flowers? The country looked so beautiful. I wanted to go. I wanted to see, but these days it's just not convenient, by which I understood he meant not safe. Was he a good guy? A bad guy? I don't know. He was a man who missed his country even while he was living in it. And we ate dinner at night surrounded by this vision of all the places we couldn't go. The beautiful Guatemala inside Guatemala.

Rudy laughs when I tell him. "Cati, he means Guatemala City."

They said, Of course we'll never have children. But I rescued Kitty and left my sister. It would have made more sense to say we'll never have a cat, and we don't. Rudy fills a space for me somewhere between human and feline. By which I mean the attachment exists without words, without English or Spanish, what we communicate best is simply the comfort of each other's presence.

So when Rudy takes the day off, April 22, and we drive up to Lancaster, though there's a lot we maybe could, maybe should, say, I know we may ride in silence or stick to observations like how his Honda needs a visit to the car wash. Dirt smears on the windows refract light into rainbows on the glass, an overlay of color on the hills, quarries, construction sites as we travel north.

"Lancaster for your anniversary?" Drea couldn't believe it. The northern desert end of the county, not a place anyone we know would go. "Whatever for?"

"The poppies are in bloom."

Kira will have a playdate with Vanessa till Tony picks her up to spend the night. Rudy and I will hike through fields of flowers where there's even a State nature reserve. Dinner together at a steakhouse where we can enjoy red meat without offending our daughter. A motel room. Privacy!

And a world that isn't urban or suburban. We make our sociological observations. New housing developments in the middle of nowhere but the homes are squeezed tight together. "How else can you afford to bring in electric and water?" Rudy says.

Stacked slabs of rock that look like fungi growing slant on a fallen tree. The roadside sign says Vasquez Rocks.

"You think that's Vasquez as in Tiburcio Vásquez?" Kira was writing about him for Los Angeles history. Rudy's lived here longer than I have, but I still feel called upon to instruct him. How Vásquez became a folk hero and it's still not clear whether he was an ordinary bandit or freedom fighter against the Anglos.

Even Rudy's "hmmm" has an accent, coming out more like a grunt. And on I chatter. His wedding ring shines, more golden than the one on my finger. Does he take it off when he operates, and then clean it, polish it? My father never wore a wedding ring, not that he was one of those men who cheat, as far as I know, but one who said Men don't wear jewelry, nothing beyond a simple wristwatch, cufflinks if called for, a tie clasp.

Tiburcio Vásquez, on the other hand, was a dandy, known for his fancy dress and lots of women. "We're so damn weird. Hang a man as a bandit and then name a park after him. Romanticize an outlaw."

"How is the boy?" Rudy asks.

The outlaw.

"Javi has a hearing next week to decide if he'll be tried as an adult."

"Will you go?"

"Not allowed," I say. "And the doctors won't discuss his case with me. I care about him but that doesn't give me any rights. You treated him. They might talk to you."

He grunts.

"Why did Javi get to you?" I ask.

Rudy stares straight ahead out through the windshield. "Guatemalan. I could tell he wasn't Mexican or Salvadoran. I knew he was Guatemalan."

"So? You've treated Guatemalans before," I say without saying You're the man who chose to leave his homeland far behind and not look back.

The house Rudy grew up in, as far as I know, still stands, but it's as though his whole country was lost to fire. His family scattered. His parents and one sister in Mexico, a brother in Paris, another brother now trying to make his way in Spain. Rudy chose our daughter's name, spelled with a "K," a letter the Spanish alphabet only borrowed for foreign words, and pronounced to rhyme with Ira, Myra, where a Spanish-speaker would say Keera. A man I've never understood but I know would die for our daughter and very likely would give his life for me.

"Once he's out of the hospital," I say, "they lock him up. I think as soon as he's of age they ship him back." Our other form of extraordinary rendition. We fly gang members to Guatemala, El Salvador, where they receive the official welcome: a bullet in the head. "If he survives, he'll look for his mother." And what are the chances he can find her? I looked up the population of Guatemala City. Some reports say 2,541,581. A different census says 1,150,452. There are at least 500,000 people in the shantytowns, but no one has really managed to count. His mother is surely among the uncounted. The number keeps growing in El Mezquital, Tecún Umán, Balcones de Palín, which we might as well call the Guatemala inside Guatemala, which is very much like the Los Angeles inside Los Angeles, where kids like Javi are always in the headlines even as they remain unseen. And if he finds her? Will she even believe he is her son? Can even a mother love a face like Javi's?

"He keeps asking What's going to happen to me? And it's crazy--I think he's doomed, but at the same time it makes me giddy with happiness that he's actually thinking about his future."

Rudy says nothing.

I say, "You should go see him."

The hideous boy. His shaved head, the tattoos on his neck now camouflaged by scarring, his bandages bright against his damaged skin, the pressure garments muted like a fog on his damaged legs. Angry colors, the red and purple, the bruise colors, the black, the brown that looks like leather, the waxy rinds of white showing beneath the brown. His sma̲ ̲s the grafts shrink and tighten. His patient explanations, th̲.̲.̲ p̲.̲.̲.̲.̲.̲ ̲.̲.̲.̲.̲, ̲.̲.̲ ̲.̲.̲w of the street, it's just the way things are, and those dark eyes, hurt, defiant, looking at me with suspicion and a small very tentative hope. Which is different from optimism. You hope in spite of.

And I want to take him home and I want to shield him from his laws and the law of the gang and the law of the state, from the nurse with her suspicions and the cop at the door. I want to take him back to his birth, to his infancy, to before the abandonment and the violence and start the story over, with reasons to be hopeful.

"We could become foster parents," I say. "We could even adopt him."

Rudy says nothing.

I want to put my arms around that child. If I could take him home, I think I could hug a boy who's probably too old to accept a mother's hugs.

"Or just, if he can get out on bail, maybe for a weekend?"

Rudy says, "He will not be under the same roof as Kira." And isn't this why I married him? Because I knew he would protect our children. "No." He says it with the same finality as when Tony brings him petitions to sign expressing outrage after the latest atrocity in Guatemala. "I still have people there. No."

"Why did you get me involved?" I ask.

He says, "I don't know."

We exit the freeway and travel west. There's a sign for Mira Loma. "Rudy, that's the detention center for immigrants." It was in the news. Journalists weren't allowed inside, Amnesty International was denied access to the prisoners. The men lay down in the yard and spelled out the word HELP with their bodies for the news helicopters flying overhead. They got on TV. They didn't get help. "Where is it? That building behind the animal shelter?" Or further on, what looks like a derelict prison, razor-wire fence surrounding little more than dust. "Is that where Javi will go?"

"I don't know," Rudy says. "There must be someplace else for children."

Someplace just as bad, I think. How can they do this? They can do anything to an immigrant these days. All over the country, agents raid factories. They burst into homes in the middle of the night. The knock on the door. Your papers, please. They board buses and trains and take away anyone with a Spanish accent or Latino look. They took a man from El Salvador even though he was legal. They beat him, threw him to the ground, detained him and released him in the end without an apology. They could take Rudy. It's not like he carries his naturalization papers with him, but then Rudy doesn't ride buses. So much for global warming. If you have an accent, you better stick to your car.

Five miles to the reserve and we already see poppies growing wild. Outside Rudy's window, a pasture with must be more than a hundred sheep, no fence, only one lazy sheepdog stretched out by the road watching the cars. On my side, a few nuns in gray habits scamper over a carpet of flowers.

"A Sound of Music sequel?" I ask Rudy.

The poppies are the orange color of traffic cones, some with bright yellow tips. We come around a curve and see the hills. I call my husband's name. Turn the car around. I can't do this. Hills glowing orange, as if in flames.

Rudy makes a sharp U and we head back the way we came, past sheep and nuns. There's a vertical wall of mountain to the south and to the southeast, snowcapped peaks. Then we hear the sirens. The blue sky fills with smoke. The windows are up but the chemical taste comes in—not smoke after all but teargas. My skin burns, my eyes sting. Something is happening at Mira Loma. Police cars block the road—twenty, thirty, forty. We're coughing. Noses running. Gas coats our throats. Rudy hands me a water bottle. "Rinse your mouth out. Don't open the door." He hands me a plastic bag. "Cough. Spit." Something bad is happening to the men behind barbed wire. Rudy takes off his glasses. His eyes are red and wet. The gas does what it's supposed to do. We cry.

Even in a cheap motel on Sierra Highway there's more pillows than we know what to do with. Rudy holds me for a long time and then I realize it's me holding him as he tells me about the budget cuts. The ER and the entire trauma unit will be shut down. Which is like shutting down Rudy's American identity. "But–" I begin and it's already too late. Rudy is asleep.

I can't sleep. I still have the chemical taste in my mouth and I'm thinking about hospitals closing. Drea will be pleased. She hates it that someone like Javi gets free care even though I argued we sort of owe him. We foment war in his country, we deport his mother, we leave him to the streets. And I think about teachers being laid off. Tony expects a pink slip. I'm thinking about the war, and about so much going wrong at once, a fire blazing out of control. People inside barbed wire. "But they're illegal," Drea says. And I say, "How can it be a crime if they get none of the rights guaranteed a criminal?" I always have an answer for her, but what do I know? I know nothing. I forgot my sister in the burning house. With no answer, all I have is grief.

Tell the Americans. Tell the people in your country. How naïve those people were and so was I. No somos libres. I held onto that note not knowing it was my country that supplied the money, the ideology, the training, the green light for the killings, and the guns. I held it proudly because I represented my country. I stood for the very light of freedom.

Sunlight comes through one small gap in the drapes and spills over Rudy's body, the scratches I left on his back. He's so skinny these days. I need to feed him better. And he's exhausted. Rudy drinks Coke at all hours, even for breakfast, but never in front of Kira. The coffee at the hospital is awful and he always needs caffeine and now he won't have to complain anymore about bad hospital coffee. He snores so lightly, it can hardly be called a snore, ladylike, quiet, like a cat. In English cats have nine lives, in Spanish, gatos have only seven. And people? Merry didn't even get a whole life. This country gave my husband his life number two. When the ER closes will he find a third? There he is now, asleep on his side, holding onto his ribs. Ay, Rudy! Whoever you are in secret inside, you are mi vida.

Something else that Rudy, Tony, and I have in common: We say we care but we go so far and no further. We get involved in people's lives just for a while.

We like a good dramatic story but prefer not to know how it ends. Rudy, obviously, in the trauma unit, matters of life and death. Me, summarizing depositions without paying attention to who the people are or how much they have at stake. Tony used to teach high school, but too many kids he cared about ended up killing someone or getting killed. Now he chooses second grade so the kids he loves are out of his view before much of anything can happen.

I go to see Javi. They say he'll be discharged soon and I want to hug him though I'm sure it's already too late.
Scar tissue turns his flesh to wood.
"Touch me," he says.
If the nurse comes in, I'll probably be charged with sexual abuse, but I do.
"I see your hand touching me," he says. "But I don't feel nothing."
I touch his face, his arm. I touch his leg.
A tear runs down his cheek. He most likely can't feel it, maybe just its heat as it leaves his good eye.
I touch his throat. What will become of him? After he goes to court, I wonder if I'll ever see him. If I'll even try.
"Nothing," he says.
I run a finger around his ear.
I put a hand inside his gown, upon his chest, and Javi cries out.
"I feel that, Miss," he says. "I feel."

"Since Bush?" I tell Drea. "It's about looting the government. Tax the working class to pay off the rich. Privatize so their cronies can turn public services into profit centers. Of course it started with Reagan. That's when the Great Society became the Greed Society."
"Which worked out very well for us," Drea says.
Yes, Rudy's a board-certified surgeon. He'll find work and this time, far from the 'hood, he'll be paid well. We'll give Kira everything a child can need. And any advantage a parent can imagine.
Kira and Vanessa climb into the backseat. If it weren't such a bumper-sticker slogan, I would ask them to imagine a better world.

Children should have unrestrained imaginations but my sister and I had none, at least when it came to names. We were literal thinkers, Merry and I. We called our cat Kitty. Even our imaginary world–a parallel universe under the spotted linoleum of our shared room–was simply called The Children's Land. It was a place with no parents, where we could do whatever we wanted to do. Merry and I gorged on ice cream, rode zebras bareback, climbed into swan boats so we could float down sparkling rivers and beneath waterfalls that greeted us with rainbows and trees that dropped candies into our laps in a place filled with the perfume of every kind of flower, blooming in every single color without a single bee. Our boat docked at a landing where a treasure chest waited and we plunged our greedy arms into piles of diamonds and dollars and gold. We filled our pockets. Why? Here where all was given, what use was money? Grownups prized it. We lived inside their world though what that meant was more than we could yet imagine. Why did we take all we could carry? In The Children's Land, everything was free. Everything and everyone--free.

MICHAEL SALCMAN

IF A YOUNG MAN SHOULD DIE ALONE

If a man dies alone in the sophisticated West
who will say mass or sing Kaddish for him?
Oh sure, an uncle may erect a stone
or a sister serve wine and quince pie at a wake
but that won't shake the loneliness out of the grave.

In far-off Xi'an,
where an entire army lies buried with its emperor
and a bachelor's estate is considered a disgrace,
die young and the farmers will do more for your soul
than pray, they will build you a bride.

If your family has cash and her dowry gets paid
they'll dig up a coffin and pronounce you engaged.
Of course you must hope that a good match has been made,
a slim one who's just died from boredom or plague
or a girl fished from the river with lips on her face.

Then the neighbors will gather in song
as the yellow dust falls. Even if no one in Gansu can pay,
a straw bride must be made so they can party and slaughter a pig
in your honor. *What a nice-looking couple*, your parents will say,
before sending you off on your connubial way

JANE SADEK

COVERED LADIES

I see them in my neighborhood supermarket.
At first glance,
A hint of mystery and allure
From a distant oasis.
I yearn for the different and the faraway
As I stand among pinto beans and margarine.
The moment passes
And I hear point of sale advertisements
Yammer away above my head;
"Eat smart, save money and buy my brand."

When did the local grocery store become a supermarket anyway?
My dad served as grocer and butcher in Melissa, Texas
Before World War II turned him into a trainer for B-26
bombardier-navigators.
He offered fresh meat, vegetables,
Bulk staples and a selection of canned foods
In a small downtown storefront.
Dad knew all of his customers,
Carried most of them on credit
And played dominos with the old guys when he could.
No need for grocery carts or point of sale advertising.
The mere idea of self-serve aisles would have filled the store with laughter.

My memories of the local grocery store,
In Little Rock, Arkansas, during the late Fifties,
Feature concrete floors, cramped aisles and paper bags.
In McKinney, Texas, during the Sixties,
Grocery bags were still paper,
But the aisles widened, linoleum tiles covered concrete,
And chrome gleamed;
But pharmacies, delis, bakeries and florists belonged to the future.
No one asked if you needed help with your bags—
A nice man, like my Uncle Garvis,
Who worked for Jimmy White's Humpty Dumpty
All of his life,

Rolled the cart out and put your groceries in the trunk,
Carefully securing the bags.

When making her weekly trip to the grocery store,
Mother replaced her housedress and apron
With a crisp shirtwaist dress or soft blouse and skirt.
My sister and I would get a 'wash off' and fresh clothes.
As Mother checked our nails and combed our hair,
She explained, "We'll see people you know.
Always look neat and clean,
When you go out,
So others will understand you are nice people."
Mother shopped from a list
Laboriously prepared from consultations
With store circulars from the newspaper,
Recipes in her red and white checked Betty Crocker cookbook,
And the inventory in her pantry, deep freeze and refrigerator.
We saw people we knew as we wandered the aisles:
Ladies that lived on our street or around the corner,
Ladies that worshipped at our church,
Ladies that attended high school with Mother
Or whose husbands worked with Dad,
But no covered ladies.

Now, as I go to the supermarket
Several times a week
Dressed in anything
To grab items off the shelf
Without the benefit of a list
Created from ads in newspapers I do not take
Because I use the internet for news,
I see the improvements:
A bank,
A produce department with artificial rainfall
Preceded by softly rumbling thunder,
Plastic sacks instead of paper bags,
Conveyor belts instead of checkout counters,
Computer terminals and scanners
Instead of grand cash registers
With their impressive rows of numbered buttons.

Sullen teenagers, in serial cameo appearances,
Unceremoniously dump piles of thin sacks,
Each with a minimum of four items, into the carts.
Then the teenager may ask if you want help to your car
As he walks to the next check stand.
Or you may help yourself on the self-service aisle,
While a harried clerk tries to satisfy the stares
Of six angry customers with anonymous machines
Beeping erroneous messages.

At the supermarket
I don't see a soul I recognize,
But I see the covered ladies
Arriving in a wide variety.
Some ladies, covered from head to toe in black
With mesh over their eyes
And long sleeves to cover their hands,
Are brought to the supermarket in the evening
By their husbands, who entertain the children
While offering commentary on the groceries selected.
They remind me of an article in my *Aramco World* magazine.
The author talked of her devotion to Allah,
Of the security provided by her culture and her veil,
Of the respect and honor earned.
Other covered ladies come alone with their children,
Admonishing them to obedience, in tones I recognize
Even though the words are not familiar.
Their long dark robes fall in folds to the floor,
But the sleeves do not cover the hands.
Beautifully woven headdresses in subtle dark tones
Frame faces I am allowed to see.
I understand these women,
Holding on to a culture dear to them,
Though different from mine,
Trying to make a traditional belief fit into a modern world.
I pity the necessity of heavy robes in Texas heat
Though I know their homelands may be even warmer.
I even consider the possibility that their headdresses
Could be promising solutions to my frequent bad hair days.
I saw a woman wrapped traditionally from head to toe,

But instead of a heavily woven robe of a single color
And a headdress of somber tones,
Her robe and headdress were covered in roses the color of butter
And the material floated in the wind, like silk.
A small girl in a tiny bikini,
Festooned in pink and purple rickrack,
Stood by her side.
I wonder what traditions or compromises
Separate her from the other covered ladies.
I see young women wearing tight jeans and even tighter t-shirts,
The closefitting encasement more enticing than modest,
And on their heads, the woven scarves of their mothers.
What do all these covered ladies think of each morning,
As they carefully fashion the draping folds of their scarves,
Which separate them from me?

I want to believe the covered ladies are here for freedom's sake,
The veil a choice they made for themselves.
I want to believe they honor my choice as I honor theirs,
Yet I must wonder.
Nabil told me of his boyhood in Egypt,
When it was rare to see the covered ladies.
Muslims and Christians mixed in the street
And around the dinner table
As if religion were a simple preference,
Like choosing a blue car instead of red.
Yet each family honored their own beliefs
With as much respect as they honored their neighbors'.
While Nabil lived in America, something changed.
During visits to his family, he noticed women huddled in the streets,
Shrouded in huge scarves covering dark dresses,
Eyes downcast, never smiling.
Later his family reported hijabs replacing scarves,
And abayas, dresses.
As I planned for a visit to Egypt,
My Coptic in-laws said, "Bring blouses that cover your arms.
Pack pants, not shorts, and skirts that are long.
Do not wear bright colors, or anything sheer. You must dress as we do."
Still, they were relieved when the airline lost my luggage,
Allowing them to dress me from their own closets.

In spite of this, as I shopped for souvenirs in the Khan Il Kalili,
A Muslim man handled me familiarly and ran away laughing.
In my shock, I complained to Nabil, but regretted it in fear,
As I held his arm begging him to stay,
Not to chase the man because we were foreigners
Even though Nabil felt he was at home.
Back at the flat, the family told me
Their somber clothes are not a part of their own religion or desires,
But are worn to avoid conflict and insult,
Which often come, in spite of their efforts.
Their photos from the Sixties revealed scenes in Cairo
Resembling the Paris of those days.
Ladies in chic suits and flowing flowery dresses
Walked arm in arm with handsome men in suits and fezzes.
In one, a young Nabil stands with his sister aboard a ferry.
She wears a lovely pale suit with a fur collar and matching hat.
Mona tells me how proudly she wore them,
Walking with her fine-looking brother on a holiday outing.
Then tears come to her eyes as she tells how her daughters
Are insulted and spat upon
As they walk through the streets of the city
To and from school or church or a nearby store.
The man in the bazaar does not surprise them,
But they had hoped I would be spared.
My niece told a story about Mona,
Who teaches English in a public school in Heliopolis,
Only a year or so away from a retirement earned through much difficulty.
Her students are Muslim
Because any Copt who can afford it
Sends their children to private schools.
They wear black abayas and hajibs
Because no Christian woman is allowed to teach the males.
One day Mona came home crying
Because a student slapped her,
Mockingly calling her a useless old woman.
The girl felt no need to learn
Because her family would find her a husband
And she needed only to know how to please him.
Mona's family gathered round her.
Her husband, Mohktar, a doctor,

Was forced to give up private practice by age and politics.
And the daughter, Magy, who graduated from the university with honors
And a degree in accounting,
Could only find work as a receptionist because she is a Copt.
Mirette was not there because she is married
And lives in Sharm El Sheik,
A beautiful seaside oasis.
But there is no hope of living in Cairo,
Where her sons could enjoy their extended families
Because there is no job for a Coptic man in the city
Which would allow him to support his wife and three boys.
Bassem, Mona's beloved son, was in America.
He was lucky to have an uncle to sponsor him for a green card
Because he was also unable to find work in Cairo.
Mohktar and Magy assured Mona she was of great use
And Mona said, "I do not cry for myself,
I cry for her.
She does not long for knowledge
And will always depend on someone else.
What can the future be for her,
For all of them?"
Magy married a doctor and lives in the U.S.
Mona earned an American citizenship
And hopes she can wait for Mohktar's citizenship to move to the U.S.
Mirette's husband, lulled by freedom of the European tourists
He serves in the Thomas Cook office in Sharm,
Ignored the bomb which went off next to his office,
Perhaps because he had gotten home from work
Or perhaps because he doesn't want to see.
In Egypt, Mona cannot wear a silk dress covered in yellow roses.
And my brilliant niece with her doctor husband cannot find work
Because their identification cards list their religion next to their pictures.
Their church in Cairo
Has a restroom, locked for ten years
Because the permit required to repair it
Is classified as an improvement to the building
And is considered problematic to the government.

I want to think what happened there
Cannot happen here.

I want to believe
I will remain free to wear what I want
As the covered ladies are,
But Mona says when she was on the ferry
In her fur trimmed suit and hat,
She didn't think it would happen there, either.

MARY ZELINKA

RIDING A HURRICANE

Last year while staying alone on the Oregon Coast, late one night I walked a lonely stretch of beach. Only the moon lit my way. The tide was low and I walked out to meet it. I stood there some moments in the darkness as the ocean hovered in that in-between place before releasing its waves again. Suddenly, the sand sank beneath my feet and water seeped over the tops of my boots. I slupped one foot and then the other out of the slush, desperately seeking firmer ground. But I kept sinking and the ocean lapped cold against my shins. Panicked, I lifted my feet again and again away from the ocean until at last I collapsed on solid sand.

This is how I have felt since I learned of my father's death.

"Dad died a week ago last Friday," said my brother's email. "The funeral was Tuesday."

I squinted at the words shivering across my computer screen, finally printing out Charles's message to be sure that's what it really said. My hands shook so much I had to lay the paper down on my desk so I could read it. Only last week someone asked if my father was still living and I had responded, "I think so. We've been estranged for a few years, but my sister or brother would let me know." I had even laughed. And all the while my father lay dead.

Charles's email was in response to mine the day before. I had received a package from him. No note, just a small box rubber-banded with a slip of paper, "For Mary Helen," in my mother's spiky handwriting. The rubber band, brittle with age, cracked as I removed it. Inside was the tiny china doll, no bigger than my thumb, which had been Mother's when she was a child.

During the past months Charles had sent a number of packages: cards I had sent Mother, my elementary school report cards, paint-by-number horses. With each securely taped package, I'd smile; Mother had kept everything. Charles must be sorting through the drawers and closets crammed with her hoarding. My older sister, Gracie, made frequent trips to our childhood home in Miami and would be directing him. I hadn't been home since Mother's death five years before.

Now I cringe to think how I gushed my gratefulness over each package. I hung the 1968 Colorado license plate from the jeep I had in college in my den and took Charles's CD of pictures down to Kinko's to make prints.

My brother, five years younger than I, lived his life in a secret, hidden fashion, and I treasured each interaction.

Mother's doll had been in Father's safe deposit box; I had seen it there when Gracie and I went to the bank with him after Mother died. I emailed Charles. Was something wrong with Father? Now, here on my computer screen, was my answer.

My son, Bob, drives big rigs up in the Colorado mountains and normally I wait until I think he's home before I call. "I can't believe they didn't tell you," he said. In spite of shouting over the rattling diesel engine, his voice sounded full of concern. "Who *are* these people?"

Then I dialed my old telephone number, the same one my parents had had since 1954. I imagined the shrill ring of the kitchen wall phone shattering the thick silence. I pictured Charles slapping his magazine to the floor and lurching out of the low-slung chair in his room, his long heavy steps pounding across the marbled Cuban tile. He would have grabbed the dining room doorjamb as he swung around it to snatch up the phone, leaving smudges as he had since he was a boy. After my mother's death no one would have reminded him for the umpteen millionth time not to.

"Why didn't you or Gracie call me?" I pressed the phone hard against my ear to stop it from shaking.

"He didn't want anyone to know," Charles said, his voice brisk and efficient.

"Had he been sick?"

"Prostate cancer. He'd had it a while, but was fine, walking five miles a day. He collapsed in August."

This was January. August was four months ago. "Why didn't you or Gracie tell me? I would have come home."

"I guess you just dropped through the cracks. He didn't want anybody to know. Just family."

"I'm family," I whispered.

Charles exhaled loudly. "He told us not to call you. He didn't want you around."

My chest went cold with shame.

"I've been going through stuff and getting the house ready to sell," Charles went on as though this were a normal everyday conversation. "I mailed you Mother's glass float ball, you should be getting it any day."

His voice sounded far away, as though in a dream. I stared out at the growing darkness outside. Even from his deathbed Father had wanted no part of me.

Later that night as I was getting ready for bed I remembered Mother's glass float. Even though I wasn't with her that day, I'll never forget when she found it. It was after the hurricane in 1962. The first day the causeway to Key Biscayne reopened, she took off to walk the lonely stretch of beach to the lighthouse.

Mother spotted it from some distance away, plopped right there in the sand, bigger than a basketball. She had never heard of anyone finding a glass float on a Miami beach before, and she would know, she walked the beach every chance she got. She hid it under some palm fronds so she could continue her walk without carrying it. Mother said she practically ran all the way to the lighthouse and back she was so excited.

"Did it come all the way from Japan?" I asked that afternoon when I got home from school. I stroked the heavy green glass.

"Maybe," she said. "Or Norway or England. Glassblowers used to make floats there too. Just think! It probably bobbed around in the ocean for years before getting swished up by the hurricane." Her eyes shone with the magic of it all.

The float had sat on the floor in the living room in front of the frosted glass window crisscrossed with shelves filled with seashells. As I lay in the darkness willing sleep to come, I wondered what would become of Mother's shell collection. She had taught me to love the ocean too and most of my own shells had been presents from her.

The next morning I called Charles again. "I'd like to have Mother's triton shell."

Charles sounded irritated. "I don't even know what a trident is."

"Triton. It's about thirteen inches long, brown and orange speckled. It used to sit on Mother's desk." I could picture her hand resting absently on it as she talked on the phone.

"I'll look, but I don't know. There's a lot of stuff around here." At that moment I realized Charles thought his responsibility to me was done when he mailed off the glass float.

I took a deep breath. "Charles, do you know if Father took me out of his will?"

"Look, all I know is he was very angry at you. I don't know about the will. Talk to Gracie."

My chest went tight. After mother died Gracie had made it clear she no longer wanted to talk to me. We hadn't spoken in almost five years. But suddenly it seemed imperative that I know whether my father had truly stopped loving me. I dialed the number Charles gave and held my breath.

When Gracie came to the phone I told her I had been afraid she wouldn't talk to me.

"Why?" she asked as though nothing were wrong.

I hesitated. "Because I never hear from you. And you didn't let me know Father died."

"But I never hear from you either," she said in that singsong voice we had taunted one another with as children.

I shook my head, trying to make sense of this quavery new world I seemed to have sunk into. "I wish you had called me when Dad got sick."

"Oh, well, it was so hard. He was in a lot of pain. As his Appointed Personal Representative, as they call it in Florida, I felt honor bound to uphold his wishes."

"I wish you had called."

"Kay was going to, but I guess she's been busy with her two little ones."

It wasn't your daughter's job to call me, I thought. It was yours. Or Charles's.

I could see this conversation wasn't going to go anywhere. "Gracie, did Father write me out of the will?"

Gracie was quiet for a minute. "Charles is going to be so mad at me for telling you. Yes. He did. He told us about the screaming match the two of you had."

Of course Father would have referred to our last conversation as a "screaming match." No one ever crossed him and got away with it. My words, though spoken barely above a whisper, still echoed in my head: "You may not speak of my son or grandson in this manner. I can no longer talk to you."

"You should be receiving a copy of the will in a week or two," Gracie went on. "There should be something in there about contesting if you want to."

It didn't occur to me until after we hung up that Charles had lied; he knew about the will. I wondered if they had planned for me to learn of Father's death through the paperwork from his attorney. Tears prickled my eyes; I would never again get to leaf through my father's photography books or examine the miniatures Mother had stockpiled for the dollhouse she would build someday.

This made the second time that I'd been disinherited by my family.

The first time was long before my mother died. I remember telling my therapist, "Being left out of the will isn't about the money. It's just that

I'm one of their children too and I want to be acknowledged as being part of the family."

"But it is about money," she replied. "A will is the way your parents take care of you after they are gone. Your parents place a very high value on money. Withholding it means withholding love."

She held my eyes as we sat in the stillness of her office, my heart suddenly racing ahead of the clock's measured tick, tick, tick. I thought back to my childhood when my various crimes, such as failing a spelling test or talking back to Mother, had resulted in being grounded and worse, my parents' shunning. Mother turning her back to me in disappointment. Father's disgusted shake of his head. Their days-long silences. I repented by remembering to make my bed in the morning, washing the dishes without being told, and doing my homework. Finally they would resume speaking and life returned to normal. Each time I'd silently vow to never ever do anything again to make my parents stop loving me.

The first time my parents disinherited me was in 1979 when I gave up custody of Bob to his father, my first husband. My second husband had battered me until I couldn't think straight and convinced me that Bob would be better off without me. "This is wrong, wrong, wrong!" Mother had written in a special delivery letter. "You are abandoning your child!"

Surely they would understand and forgive me if they saw me, I thought. So after I sold my house in Colorado, I drove clear to Miami before heading off to Oregon where I intended to start a new life. I pulled into the driveway late at night after three days of hard driving. Father looked up from his workbench as I walked into the garage on my way into the house. His face went dark. "What are *you* doing here?"

I stayed two days, but he didn't speak to me again.

Mother could barely look at me. "It must be nice driving around the country in a new van, all footloose and fancy free. Maybe I should have given away my children too!" And then, as if I hadn't already figured it out, "You are no longer part of this family."

But several months later after I got to Oregon, Mother and I started talking. Realizing that I had already done the worse thing I could possibly do in her eyes, I didn't hide anything in our phone conversations. She knew I was involved with a married man and she knew I sometimes drank too much. She told me she missed the beach; now that Father had retired she rarely got out of the house except to go to the grocery store. "I hate not knowing what the storms have left behind!"

A couple of years after my move to Oregon, desperate to go home once more, I flew to Miami for Christmas. Other than a "pass the salt," my father didn't speak to me and without the safety of the whole country between us, Mother and I were shy with one another. We kept our conversations clear of any intimate talk. I told her about my work at the Center Against Rape and Domestic Violence and the shelter we had just opened.

The afternoon before I left, Mother called me into the living room. "I think I understand now why you left Jack and gave up Bobby," she said, her eyes filling with tears. "Can you ever forgive me for acting so ugly to you?"

Mother had never before admitted to me she was wrong. My knees buckled and I sank into the couch. Tears sprang from my eyes. "I don't know if I can," I cried. "It was so hard! I had to start all over again in Oregon where I didn't know anybody. All I had left was my dog Beau Beagle." I reached for a kleenex and swiped it over my eyes. "You accused me of abandoning Bobby. But at least I sent him to his dad. It was you who abandoned me!"

We sat there weeping, staring at each other for some minutes. Finally, her eyes glistening red with sorrow, Mother whispered, "I hope someday you can forgive me."

It took me a few weeks. That awful time was buried deep within me and forgiving her meant I would have to dig it out and mold this new piece around it. When I finally phoned her we cried and told each other all of our secrets.

Father did not ask for my forgiveness. But the next year at Christmas he looked at me across the dinner table one night when I was relating a story about Beau Beagle, and said, "The two of you have been through so much together." It was the most intimate thing I had ever heard my father say. I began fantasizing about forging a friendship with him.

But I could never pull it off. If he answered the phone when I called home, he responded to my "Hi, it's me Mary," with "I'll get your mother."

Even with Mother's and my closeness, I remained disinherited. "Your father and I are not going to change our will again," Mother announced out of the blue as we walked her dog during one of my annual Christmas visits. "Gracie has the Sargent portrait," referring to our sour-looking ancestor, Prudence. "And Charles will get the house. The balance of the estate will be split between them."

We stopped as Buster strained at his leash sniffing the neighbor's Hibiscus hedge. "That's very unfair," I said. "I'm one of your children too."

"You'll be fine." She reached over and took my hand. "You can take care of yourself; Gracie's never had to support herself. And it's always been hard for Charles that he wasn't able to get on with the airlines. There's nothing he wanted more than to be a pilot." She sighed. My brother still lived at home and had never held a job for more than a few months at a time.

"There's not many of us who get what we want from life," I said, thinking of my son who was being raised by his Dad and step-mother. My two failed marriages. Buster snorted at the hedge and resumed his stroll along the sidewalk.

Several years after that walk, Charles phoned saying Mother was in the hospital with collapsed lungs, a respirator stuck in her neck. I was hesitant to call Father. We had never before had a conversation, just the two of us.

When I did call, Father's vulnerability surprised me. "Boy, am I glad to hear from you!" he cried. He told me he loved me. He had never said that before. "Something happening like this makes you realize how important family is," he said when I told him I loved him too.

None of this changes the past, I thought when we hung up. But it changes everything about the future. At last Father and I could become friends.

But the next night he was too tired to talk. The night after that was the same. Then he said it would be better if I just talked to Gracie.

When Gracie and I were home for Mother's funeral, Charles committed some sin against Father and he decided Charles should be cut out of the will too. Gracie disagreed. "You have three children and we should all be included equally," she said. "If the will slants to my favor, Charles and Mary will blame me." I admired Gracie for speaking up to him.

Father already had an appointment with an attorney so Gracie drove, and I tagged along. Gracie traced her finger where he should sign, his head turned to the side as he aimed the small point of vision left from his macular degeneration at her finger. His signature officially brought me back into the family. I marveled over the influence Gracie seemed to have over him.

Now I wonder about Father's final days. If Gracie had encouraged him, would he have been willing to speak to me just once more before he died? Gracie knew what it was like being the target of Father's anger. And she would remember how hurt I had been the first time Mother and Father disinherited me. Over the years she and I had spent many hours on the phone recounting the stories. The time Father refused to let Gracie come home after she flunked out of college – condemning her to a dingy yellow apartment in the downtown Miami YWCA until she got accepted at another school. The time I gave up my best friend Linda when I was eight because Father always joked with her and he never even spoke to me. The time he took our bedroom door off the hinges and left it in the garage for two years because Gracie slammed it once too often.

Truthfully, I wasn't surprised that Father had cut me out of his will again. With Father there was no such thing as unconditional love. After that final phone conversation, I pictured him storming out of the house and marching the three miles to his attorney in South Miami, his white cane furiously beating the sidewalk. He must have cursed my name daily.

By that time Gracie had renounced me too.

The afternoon after Mother's funeral, Gracie and I had driven with Father over to Key Biscayne. My mother and I had often walked to the lighthouse together, our backs hunched as we searched out little orange whelks. I had brought some sand from the Oregon coast to scatter in view of the lighthouse.

On the way, I noticed Gracie was in the lane veering us towards town, away from the beach. "You need to be in the left lane, Gracie," I said from the back seat.

"Just shut up!" she yelled. I jumped. "You always think you are so smart!" Her eyes blazed pure hatred at me in the rear view mirror before she swerved into the left lane.

Tears pricked at my eyes. As we wound our way through the park, I realized this was exactly the way we had always behaved. Gracie yelled at me, or threw something at me, or broke something of mine, and I muffled my sobs so nobody would hear.

This is not a good way to take care of myself, I thought suddenly. I vowed that the next time she yelled I was going to stand up to her.

On the beach, as I was taking off my shoes for my pilgrimage, Gracie said, "Sorry, but I'm under a lot of stress."

"My mother just died too," I said and walked on down the beach, leaving her and Father sitting in the shade.

Afterwards, when we had dropped Father off, Gracie drove right past our hotel. "You should have told me where to turn," she said. I looked at her. Then she laughed. Things were okay between us again.

We spent the next few days sorting Mother's things. Gracie filled up trash bags with scraps of material from sewing projects dating back to the 1950's. I debated about taking a swatch of parrot-green paisley from a little A-line dress Mother made me one summer when I was in college. The dress had been 1960's short and had a scalloped neckline. I wore my first dangly gold earrings with it.

"You don't want that," Gracie said, grabbing it out of my hand and shoving it in the trash bag. I didn't, but seeing it being thrown out made my throat go tight. I picked up a half-used bottle of Mother's Wind Song cologne and inhaled deeply, then put it in the box Gracie would send me after I flew home. Gracie was staying on another week.

The morning of my flight, Gracie and I sat with her grown son Bennett in a bagel shop. As I mopped at the peanut butter I had somehow gotten on my purse, Gracie and I told Bennett tales of our childhood. "Gracie fought back and demanded to be noticed, and Charles was always getting into some kind of trouble," I told him. "I just tried to stay invisible."

On the way to Father's so I could say goodbye, Gracie decided she wanted to drive by where our aunt had lived when we were growing up. From the back seat she kept telling Bennett to turn right. But all the rights were into driveways because the street snaked along the canal.

"It must be off to the left," I said.

Suddenly the Coral Gables map whacked me in the face. "You read the map if you're so damn smart!" Gracie shouted.

I picked up the map, folded it, and took a deep breath. "I don't like it when you yell at me," I said. My heart thundered in my ears.

The back seat thumped as Gracie sat back. Her silent fury filled the car.

When we got to the house, I asked Charles if he would drive me to the airport. "Gracie is so busy with Father," I said. Gracie's eyes didn't meet mine when I left.

I cried all the way to the airport and Charles must have thought I was upset over Mother because he kept saying, "At least she isn't suffering anymore."

Two weeks after I returned to Oregon Gracie responded to my letters and emails with a phone call saying she "only wanted a superficial relationship with me from now on."

"Don't do this, Gracie!" I cried. But she had already hung up.

Months later, when I confessed the incident to Charles, he scoffed at me. "Everybody yells. Father yells. Gracie yells. That's just the way the world works."

"Not my world," I replied. "Not anymore."

When I was growing up Father yelled at all of us, and Gracie shouted at Mother, Charles and me. Charles banged his fists against the hallway wall on the way to his bedroom, hollering at the world in general. Mother and I kept quiet; she stuffed her anger into her crippled arthritic spine, and I escaped to the stables where I spent so much time the owner once asked my parents if he could adopt me. I was well trained by the time I married. When I finally got away from my second husband, I was determined not to ever again stay in a relationship with anyone who was abusive.

Yet when I told Gracie I didn't like it when she yelled at me, I never dreamed it would mean she would walk out of my life for good. I had always believed I meant as much to her as she did to me.

After Mother died, Father and I agreed that I would call him at 8:00 every Saturday morning, 11:00 his time. Though he always sounded disappointed that it was me and not Gracie, some Saturdays our conversations went okay. He snorted disgustedly when I answered "Of course I am," to his question, "You aren't one of those peaceniks protesting the Iraq war, are you?" But he mailed me a tape of an NPR radio show he had listened to.

Then after a couple of months Father stopped answering the phone, or yelled at me when he did. I woke up Saturday mornings with my stomach churning. But the worse part was how he raved about Gracie and her family. Father never mentioned my son or grandson, even if I brought them up.

After I learned my niece had a baby, I could no longer bear having my own child ignored. "How does it feel to be a great-grandfather again?" I asked that fateful Saturday morning.

"Don't get me started on that guy!" he stormed. And then he launched into a tirade, hurling accusations and ugly names.

At first I thought he was talking about one of my ex-husbands. "Who are you talking about?"

"I'm talking about that deadbeat son of yours and your worthless grandson!" His anger exploded through my kitchen phone, thick and sudden.

I started to defend them. Bob, who had been able to support himself since he was fourteen. Zachary, not even five years old, already fearless on a skateboard. But then I stopped.

"You may not speak of my son or grandson in this manner," I said, my voice barely a whisper.

Father didn't respond.

"I can no longer talk to you," I said. "I'm going to hang up the phone now. Goodbye, Father."

He said a quiet goodbye and we hung up. I opened up my sliding glass door and took a deep breath. My whole body was shaking, but I felt lighter than I had in the two years since Mother died.

A week after I learned of my father's death, Mother's glass float ball arrived. I had forgotten how heavy it was – almost six pounds. I carried it into my bedroom and sat cross-legged in the middle of my bed cradling it between my legs. Tears washed over it, and I rubbed them into the thick green glass, staring into its depths as though I could once again see my childhood.

Condolences from old family friends began to appear. "I wish we had been able to come to Miami to support you." "Gracie sent me the beautiful tribute to your Father. You were blessed." "Your father was very special. He was kind, gracious, and compassionate."

How could I respond? "I wish I had been in Miami too, but Gracie and Charles didn't tell me Father died." "Kind? Gracious? Compassionate? Are you kidding?" I wanted to blow the whistle on my family, but I was too ashamed. Instead I sent notes of thanks. It seemed my right to mourn had been somehow denied me.

I thought I was ready to see the will by the time it finally came. But the earth sank from beneath me when I saw my name, Mary Helen Zelinka, spelled out four separate times so there would be no question, not the slightest doubt, that I, and my descendants, "shall not be treated as descendants of mine." Using my full name was probably just a legality, but I was furious that he had. "Mary" is my adult name. Only people who love me have the right to call me "Mary Helen."

He had signed the will a full year after I told him I couldn't talk to him anymore. I was surprised he had waited that long. Had he hoped I would apologize? If I had, would it have changed anything between us?

I had already decided not to contest the will. Instead, I spent weeks crafting a letter to Gracie and Charles. "What have I ever done to either of you?" finally gave way to "I have many happy memories of each of you and will hold you in my heart." Then I crossed that out too because now even my favorite stories about them were tainted. In the end, the letter was short, requesting only that they include me in the settlement of the estate. I asked that they not perpetuate Father's vindictiveness and anger.

My legs shook as I stood in line at the post office. It occurred to me that this letter would end the possibility of any future relationship with Gracie or Charles. If they complied with my request they would resent me and if they didn't, what would be left between us? When the clerk affixed the return receipt cards, I suddenly felt adrift, as though my anchor had broken away and I was lost at sea.

I don't need to hear from Gracie and Charles to know their answer. If they had wanted to include me, they would have contacted me when Father died. They would have asked if there was anything I wanted of Mother's or Father's. They would have wanted me to be with them as they sorted through the more than fifty-year accumulation of stuff that filled our childhood home.

Still, it is important for me to ask. I do not wish to slink quietly from my sister's and brother's lives; I do not want them to be able to pass off their dismissal of me as simply upholding Father's wishes.

When I returned home from the post office, I went straight into my bedroom and lifted the glass float from where it had been nested in my childhood rocking chair. Hugging it to my chest, I carried it out to the living room and placed it on the floor in front of the barrister's bookcase that serves as my shell cabinet. The float fit perfectly against the curve of the giant clam filled with pine cones.

My family's culture has been washed away. There is no one left with whom I can giggle or cry over shared family memories. Gracie had acted as my interpreter when I was little; only she understood what I was saying through my stuttering. We cheered "It's Howdy Doody time!" together. We ate Karo syrup on Merita thin-sliced bread for breakfast, and under Mother's watchful eye, poked mercury with our fingers, sending it into dozens of tiny quivery balls. We ate Philadelphia Cream Cheese with a spoon, and scraped the ice from the freezer door and sucked it off our fingernails.

Together, Charles and I schemed to get him expelled from his dreaded Cotillion club, finally succeeding when I drove our jeep over the manicured lawn to pick him up. I didn't blow the whistle on him the night he and his friend Alex went around the neighborhood twisting all the car antennas into knots, causing thousands of dollars worth of damage.

I remember one Sunday afternoon during a Christmas visit a few years before Mother died. Charles and I sat in the backyard next to his old fishing boat, unused for years and now overturned in the grass. He poked at the rusty bolts with his pocket knife as we talked. Even though I came home every year, I rarely saw him. He'd mutter "good morning" into his chest and duck out of the house as soon as he woke up and not return until after dinner. I asked Mother once where he went all day, but she said she had never asked. "Maybe the Parrot Jungle. I buy a pass for him every year."

I felt special that afternoon sitting in the wide-bladed grass with my brother. After a while Father walked by and said, "That's the wrong tool to use for removing bolts."

"I'm just fooling around."

Father's face went red with anger. "When you want to know how to do it right, then come into the garage and I'll show you!"

Charles shrugged his shoulders as Father stomped off. We went on with our conversation, though now Charles didn't meet my eyes.

How long could you be spoken to like that before you believed you couldn't do anything? Maybe this was why Charles had never moved out. That Sunday afternoon I had wondered for the first time if maybe my parents' disinheritance had been the best thing that ever happened to me.

It's possible that Gracie and Charles believe I abandoned them. Gracie may have thought I "turned on her." Maybe Charles believed I left him to deal with Father by himself. There would be some truth in both those perceptions. I had never before stood up to Gracie, it must have felt like an attack when I finally did. And I had indeed turned away from Father.

But I never shut the door to any of them. Father had my phone number and could have called. Gracie could have said, "I miss you. Let's make up." Charles could have asked for help. Yet deep down I know that none of them would have been able to do any of those things. So they would be right. I got out and they didn't.

This, then, is my inheritance.

That and a glass float ball, bigger than a basketball, and filled with the slow exhale of a long-ago and far-away glass blower. Severed from its fishing net, the float drifted the ocean currents for years before finally riding a hurricane to solid ground.

STEPHANIE SILVIA

Old women knitting woolen scarves

Gnarled fingers adroitly more agile than young women bejeweled beringed
Not knitting-only standing and shopping and wishing they knew how to weave
woolen shawls on a loom, like maybe their great great grandmothers did, but
thinking more about women in other countries with other cultures and no
shopping malls, who weave with wool or women in our own country, native
women who weave blankets with neatly measured patterned designs, orderly
and of mountains and rivers, geometric molecular theory on handcarded wool
from sheep on plateau.   Bejeweled bedazzled beheeled women with urges in
their fingertips wanting to warp and weft wanting to wrap themselves in silk,
raw and nubby and silk, sweet and smooth, dyed by roots and berries, red, juicy
berries, oozing sticky sweet on their hands, up to their elbows, barefooted
grape stained, vats, stomping feet in vats in some old Italy, these wanton
dreams of making bread, hands in yeast and warm squish, milk, milk, milk,
mother's milk, the memory of the suck, endless generations of baby rosebud
mouth on tender nipple and arms caressing, wanting grandmothers and
grandfathers and green hills, long grass, horses to ride to the next village.

Wanting so to crash the sky and get home to you and you and you it's been so long 3 years I have small son you have only loved once
He's ten
He plays baseball
The world is in a mess how many carbon credits to fly across the sky I buy locally but use the car a lot it's so different than NY we have to drive to almost everything (except walk dogs on the beach) (except hike up trail head to magnificent vantage point over Pacific so blue) our money is always collapsing (we don't even own a house) (we rent a double wide beneath redwoods by oceans roar)

Miss you so much nobody visited when I had cancer but I was okay and we knew it early on but still I almost bled to death in the ER—6 pints of blood, mind you, emergency surgery and still bleeding Scot rolled me from the ER to the OR, my blood dripping on the floor before his eyes. I have young son who is marvelous   6 pints of blood and radiation and nobody visited from back east but soon after we knew I would be alright just a waiting game until final surgery and cancer out out be gone it was it is I will get on plane spend all our savings for living in the summer when Scot is waiting to be paid in the fall and the school is closed and you know I can't get a teaching job here—none—but I am an hourly wage teacher's aid and we can't collect unemployment in the summer although we are hourly and get no benefits—the school is closed, no work the job is seasonal like fishing, like Scot, but we, aides, can't get unemployment anyhow (California is falling apart) good thing I got cancer and Med-I-Cal when I did before the impending doom fallout and nobody visited but I am okay so it doesn't matter I mean for real, how can it matter to me, now—   I am checking for airfares on the internet credit card in my hand I am ready to come home.

b'klyn
from the window of the D train
big houses with big trees
and long cars (a decade old)
sit in driveways next to backyards
with bird baths and baby pools

where Jews and Italians
lived side by side in neighborhoods
whose children did not date
except for stolen kisses beneath the
boardwalk at Muscle Beach
only seeing black people serving
steamers at Lundy's on Saturday night
except for the Bohemian youth
that made it over the river
to the Village or Harlem to
listen to jazz

Brooklyn the birthplace of Diane Di Prima
the birthplace of Muriel, my mother
of Linda, my aunt and me

I want to wear an African hat
woven of African colors
so I may say, "Yes, I too, have lived in Brooklyn."

I want to look at the walrus with gray whiskers and
big tusks while my grandfather holds my child hand
and plays pinochle at his Hebrew Club in Coney Island

I want to grow up and not be poor—anymore—
to go to college in Manhattan and marry a man
who will buy a house with fruit trees in the yard in New Jersey

I want to watch myself
Blossom into painful womanhood in the
mirror above the wash basin like
Francie Nolan while my handsome Irish
father sings drunken Irish songs

I want to mix praying to Catholic saints with
lighting Shabbos candles on Friday nights
On Shabbat
not driving in my father's old Falcon
not riding the D or the F train
but walking to Mermaid Avenue
to say the same prayers on the beach
that my great grandparents recited in Hebrew
and Yiddish on the steppes
as people speak in Hindu, in Spanish
and Guyanese and Chinese along the shore
all facing the Great Atlantic Mother
thanking both g-d and g-ddess
for such yearning and hope.

MATTHEW CARIELLO

STONE MAN SPEAKS

Meditations on an Inuit Figure

Stone Man Watches Fire

The world is mostly
water, but drop
me in the flame
and I won't burn,
I won't even sing.
Fire burns only
what can't keep,
and burning,
sends it away.
At the heart of it
I'll stand, barrel-chested,
my shoulders square
with the hearth.
I'll grow red as blood.
In the morning
you'll dig me
from the ashes,
smiling, and reach
for my perfect, smooth
skin, and my burning
light will caress
and wound you.

Stone Man Sleeps

I dreamed hands
tended to my body,
rubbed me clean
with oil from their skin,
shined me with
the fur of a seal,

and set me facing east.
When the sun rose
my shadow grew long
and strode across the snow.
There I found a man,
whose body of flesh and blood
had melted into light.
Seeing the shadow
I threw, his eyes
rolled back in his head,
but his hands
grasping my shoulders
shone like stars.

Stone Man Wants a Mate

Wear me in your belly
and I will keep you warm.
Nurtured, I nurture.
Borne, I bear.
I watch your sleep
and fire your dreams.
My unbroken form
is a solid longing
for your love.
I am the echo
of your mortality.
While you live,
I will flourish.
When you die,
I will grow silent,
introspective, and
keep your house
forever.
I am your twin,
your lover,
elemental.
I spell your fears.
I live your life.

Stone Man Watches Snow

I too was once buried
in the sameness of my fellows,
but now I am singular.
I was plucked from the earth.
I was carved by the mind
of a man, then by
his hand tossed
across the sea.
My weight keeps me
here on the ground,
completely surrounded
by only myself.
Deathless mineral,
I have been subsumed
into time, at the heart
of the weather, yet
removed.
The snow goes where it will,
the trees bend
in the wind,
break and die.
But I am not rooted,
not part of the earth anymore.
Snow, dirt, rock.
Flesh, earth, stone.
My place is set
among the fractured
crystals of drifting stars.

Stone Man Sees the Moon

My mirror, my mother,
sky-opal – is this
the womb from which
I dropped? Is this
my father's face?
My head is eternally

Uplifted – am I
listening to you?
Are you looking for your children,
pulling the envelope
of the sea constantly
from its rocks,
searching the black crevices,
leaving on the waters your likeness?
You come big over the sea
and mountains every day,
then diminish and sink
pitifully. I am here!
See me and I will
leap into your light –
stone for stone,
planet for planet.
I stand waiting.
Your light burns
my face and
whispers over
the cold boulders of the earth.
So much mist –
so much to block my way.

Stone Man Listens

Mute, polished ice,
burnished stone.
I alone am both silent
and still.
In me flow the colors
of the sea,
transfixed,
permanent, level
with the ocean surface.
In me swells
the hurricane wave,
hard and unloving.

But it will not fall.
I am a sure weight –
I am stone
but will not sink
or float or settle
on the earth's bed.

Again, I am lifted
in the man's hand,
brought into the light
and held to his face.
He is whispering.
What are these words?
What is my life to him?
Beyond all this,
my crystalline breath
contracts, sharpens,
and in me explode suns.

R.E. HAYES

BE WHITE WITH ME

On the car radio, it's an oldie, the Pointer Sisters yearning for a lover with a slow hand. The song ended and now there's something on about a shooting. Gwen guided the wheel with one hand and glanced over at a stack of CDs on the passenger seat, considering Nina Simone's "To Be Young, Gifted and Black"or maybe "Mississippi Goddam." On second thought, she dropped the idea and returned both hands to the wheel. Can't drive and fool with CD's too.

Today, time just turtled by. Palpable as a slight fever. Gwen wants to go home now and stop thinking. Unwind and shake off the meager accomplishment blues. On the Eisenhower Expressway, rush hour traffic is bumper to bumper. One finger darted to the classical station button and soon she felt herself swaying in the seat, humming along to Verdi's "La Donna e Mobile," ta-ra-ra-boom-tee-a, ta-ra-ra-boom-tee-a, ta-ra-ra-boom-tee-a.

The descending sun had cloaked the horizon in translucent sheets of blazing saffron. God and her friends slowly bringing down the curtain on another gorgeous spring day. Switching to a different station, the six o'clock news is on. Someone had shot a cop on the north side, in a supermarket near Wrigley Field.

"That's Sherman's store," she blurted out to the dashboard, steering the metallic-blue Volvo S80 toward the exact change lane. Fishing for coins, she narrowly missed a prominent yellow and black cement stanchion.

Karen Sherman, a drawn and thin checkout clerk, liked to brag that her cousin Derek had once played keyboards for a famous rocker band. But after an incident in Thailand, triggered by Derek's deviate libido, his face now stares out from FBI wanted posters, and TV talking heads have trained an unflattering spotlight on the B-list celeb. Sherman complained that male employees, reacting to her cousin's notoriety, were sexually harassing her. Phoning and leaving disgusting lip smacking sounds on her machine and tracing XXXs in the dirt on her red Honda Civic in the store parking lot. She suspected one or more of the younger stock-boys. "If I have to quit, I'll sue," she vowed, with a flip of her bone straight, ditch-water brown hair.

Leaving the expressway, exiting off Harlem Avenue, Gwen couldn't picture Sherman, a forty-something slip of a woman flipping out with a gun. Couldn't remember ever hearing of a female employee going postal. "Please," she begged, not in my store.

Stopping at a red light, too long. An SUV the size of Madagascar honked her forward.

She hurried by the love seat in the foyer, the corner easy chair, catching a glimpse of herself going by in the large mirror. Not waiting for the elevator, she dashed up the stairs, two flights to her 2-bedroom unit in the "village" of Oak Park, Illinois, a western burb bordering Chicago where, it is said, the saloons end and the steeples begin.

Sam's home, having used a personal day to watch Wimbledon semifinals. Asking him why he roots for Venus and Serena is like asking a Jamaican why he worships Bob Marley. "Big babe tennis," Sam calls it. He and Serena share the same muscular build, the same dark chocolate complexion, though he's taller and unquestionably slower of foot. In the car, she had wondered whether the Pointer Sisters would so brazenly pine for some slow loving if they had a man like Sam. But even so, when she looks at Sam with an uncritical eye, outside the bedroom, she sees before her an extra-large unfinished canvas, with imperfections galore. And before any talk of marriage, some issues need ironing out. *Look at Michelle Obama, she didn't settle, so why should I?*

"Sam," she cried out, slightly breathless, cell phone in hand.

Seconds later, his bodacious fourteens came plodding down the carpeted hall. The previous owner had laid wall-to-wall carpet over hardwood floors. Gwen wants to rip it all out.

"Hey baby, what's up?"

"A shooting in the Winthrop Street store."

"When?" He planted a kiss on the cheek that went unacknowledged.

"Just now on the radio."

Falling on the sofa, Gwen removed her left earring, a small gold hoop, and hit speed dial. She hoped someone answered the phone and not the recording reminding shoppers they always saved more on double coupon day. Newly appointed vice-president for Midwest labor relations, Gwen had recently put in three mind-numbing hours at the store investigating the Sherman complaint.

"Bring it on," said the brassy male voice on the other end.

She frowned, picturing Bush-Cheney-Rumsfeld; who in their right mind would answer on the company line that way?

"Yes, and to whom am I speaking?" With a pen, she made a scribbling motion in the air. Sam hurried out and quickly returned with a yellow legal pad.

Silence on the line.

"Are you an employee?"

"Nope."

"The police?"

"Nope."

"Then why are you on the store phone?"

"You sure ask a lotta questions, Miss Prissy. Are we on *Jeopardy*? Ha!"

"Who *are* you?"

"Who am I? You talking to me? You talking to me? Baby, I'm everything in life you dream of and fear." The voice, its mellow twang, seemed non-threatening and oddly flirtatious.

More silence.

Gwen's eyes darted to Sam sitting, shifting anxiously. Men who work with their hands (he's a Navy trained electrician) and were not book smart appealed to her, sparking a dormant urge to teach which she once believed her calling. She loved opening Sam's eyes to new ideas he hadn't heard of, never mind grappled with, vigilant always against coming across as Gwen of the Enlightenment, freeing him from the shackles of ignorance.

"Are any store employees around, the police? Put someone else on the phone please."

"Hey Miss Prissy, who says you can give big Mike orders?"

He coughed twice, then a sharp noise, the phone falling or tossed onto the office counter, followed by an exploding "F" bomb.

"The cops are outside," he said, matter-of-factly, back on the line.

"Yes, yes, and it's important that I speak to them."

"Uh, look, I popped a cap on one. Dead I think."

"Popped a cap? Do you mean what I think you mean?"

"Yeah, I guess so. I shot a cop."

She listened closely to the spacing of his words. Flat and lifeless, like tough-guy movie talk. Pictured Bush, his arms out at the side, hands flexed, readying to draw imaginary twin six-shooters. The image, vivid and distressing, of a wounded policeman oozing blood on the green and white tile rose up before her. For a moment, she felt the urge to remind this Mike character of the corporate-wide program for keeping aisles clean lest the stores incur personal injury liability for slip and fall lawsuits. *A lotta good that would do.*

"Is it Michael? Or do you prefer Mike? Have you worked for us before?"

"Mike's ok. Nope, never worked here. See, I ain't exactly what you call the hiring kind. So who're you?"

"I'm the executive in charge of this store." She paused a moment deciding whether to give out her real name. "Gwen, that's all you need to know for now."

"Executive? *Sweet.* But I bet working for you ain't exactly peaches and gravy." He tittered and snorted like a self-conscious 16-year-old.

Sam stood over her, gesturing, reaching for the phone as if needing to put a stop to whatever's caused his woman's pretty face to twist so distressingly.

They met online. After a flurry of text messages and e-mails, she felt it safe to let him call. In the first phone conversation, Sam learned Gwen Hudson was an attorney. He seemed mildly impressed, but just had to let her know he'd once dated a Haitian dentist. Straight away, Gwen liked his deep Don Cornelius Soul-Train baritone. The silky business, she guessed, just a lame attempt at cleverness and it didn't discourage her. A fair start, with one thing leading to another as they hoped. Now, in addition to driving a Volvo, she has a BMW, a black man working, in beauty shop parlance.

She wrote "cop killer?" on a note and waved him toward the kitchen to call the police on his cell. Pictured this creature in the manager's office, waving a gun, terrifying her customers. Definitely bad for business.

"Mike, you actually shot . . . tell me. What happened?"

"Yeah . . . see, I'm on the way to my girl's place. I get pulled over. Look, I'm on parole, they got a warrant out for possession, wanting to send me back to the joint. The cop, he chased me in here. I didn't mean to shoot. Pointed it, yeah, but didn't mean to shoot. Just wanted him to back off. Wanted to see my girl, that's all."

Never kiss a fool and never let a kiss fool you, mama always preached. Even so, during the lean dating years, Gwen too often found herself unhappily hooked up with duds, leeches, and church-going frauds. She turned to the Internet. Registered with Craigslist, searching for a decent black man. The odds were good, but the goods were odd. One suitor, the self-proclaimed Silky Sam, showed promise, declaring that he too was down for a "meaningful long-term relationship." Quickly she e-mailed him back:

"Hi, I'm Gwen and I'm five-eight, brown skin and brown eyes. I weigh about 130 well-arranged pounds. I have dimples and people say I'm attractive. I wear my hair long, it's not as long as Allison Payne's on Channel 9. I wish. But it's all mine. Let's see, I'm 28, no children and a non-smoker, too. I'm also a light drinker but I tolerate absolutely NO drugs. I enjoy reading, mainly fiction (I like reading things that make me sad) good movies, Luther Vandross, George Benson, Kenny G for those special moments." After clicking send, she cringed over the last part. *What if he thinks I'm some hootchy-kootchy woman?*

Sam's beside her on the beige leather couch, gripping his cell, pointing and miming the syllables, "po-lice." She dashed off another note directing him back to the kitchen to find out what they should do next. Minutes later, he returned and whispered, "Try to keep him talking. Cops talking at him on the other line till he hung up."

"I'm concerned, Mike, for my employees, my customers. Has anyone been hurt?"

"All the customers booked, ran out. I just let'em go. This skinny nervous lady was in the office when I took over, said Sherman on her nametag. I made her a general. Put her in charge. Yeah, told General Sherman to march everybody out. Get it? I ain't into hostages like them A-rabs. Anyway, it's real quiet in here now Miss Gwen, just me and my lonesome."

"How about the police officer?"

"Never made it inside. Seen him go down by the mailbox out front. A plain-clothes dude. I'm sorry, straight up. Really didn't mean for none of this shit--*stuff* to happen."

"So you're all alone in there? Not planning to hurt yourself are you?" She felt relieved knowing the bleeding officer had not made a mess on the store's floor. Dimly, it occurred to her that no one in the company would want him bleeding to death outside the store either.

"No ma'am, I was a Marine," he said, with a laughing snort. "And Marines don't kill *themselves*."

Sam passed his cell to her and Gwen held it near her phone enabling the police on the other end to monitor the conversation. Sensing her dry mouth, Sam left again and returned with a raspberry-lemonade Snapple. Trying to be helpful, he maneuvered the phones while she raised the bottle to her mouth. Sam is not romantic, and Lord knows he's undereducated, but Gwen knew this going in, eyes wide open. Now, after two years, her heart has grown weary little by little from the pent up longing for something more than a slow hand. *And then there's mama, saying she's gonna call him "sin-in-law" until we get married.* Sam faces a formidable obstacle; Roweena Hudson hates Danny Glover, still, for his role in "The Color Purple."

"You really should talk to the police, Mike. You can't stay in my store forever. Let me get them on the phone." A reasonable proposition, she thought, and it's true, he can't.

"Hey, I killed a cop."

Is he boasting, or what?

"I'm a real desperado, ma'am, give'em an inch and they'll blow me away."

At times Mike can sound warm and open with that languid southern drawl, the way he drags out and softens his vowels, maybe from Virginia or North Carolina. But in a snap, it can morph into a stark and chilling tone that makes her dislike even the idea of him. She's sure it's a white voice and confident he can't tell what she is, as if it mattered.

He had stopped with the "Miss Prissy" business and, truth be told, she liked the "Miss Gwen" touch. Maybe the officer had worn a bulletproof vest, only suffered bruised ribs. Assault on a police officer, ten years tops, out on parole in six or less—his life far from over, she thought, fully aware of thinking about this criminal as if she cared.

On the balcony, the insistent patter of falling rain is giving her the jitters. Some night soon, she reasoned, this bothersome racket will again sound wind-chime pleasing. Thousands of glistening wet jewels, streaking, tumbling, colliding in the dark untroubled expanse. Every decision tonight could affect your career she heard her calculating inner voice caution. No injured customers, no injured employees, no bleeding cop on the floor. This disturbed young man has to turn himself in. She bolted up straight, grabbed a deep breath.

"We're gonna get you out in one piece," she said. "The police don't want to harm you."

"I don't know about that. But I know I'm in a world of shit. Pardon my French."

She could hear papers shuffling on the cop's end. "Mike, I have the police, Sergeant Daniels, on another phone," she announced, drawing both hands together, fingers forming a cell phone tepee. "Good news. Luckily, the officer is still alive. Intensive care, but they say he'll live." She turned up the volume on both phones.

Sergeant Daniels spoke for the first time. "How are you doing today, Michael?"

"So, wow, you sicced the cops on me," he said. "Thanks a million."

"This is really serious, Mike. I mean, what did you expect?"

"Expect? Be white with me, Miss Gwen. That's all I expect."

She'd never before heard that odd expression, her mouth opened but nothing came out.

"Take it easy son," Sergeant Daniels said. "You *did* put an officer down, a damn good man. Like the lady said, luckily he's still with us. Aggravated assault on an officer *is* a pretty serious offense. I know you—"

"Cops outside. Cops on the phone. Whatcha-gonna-do-when-they-come-for-you. Ain't that how it goes sarge? Sarge, be honest now, you're looking for a little payback, right?"

"Michael--Mike, I wouldn't use that counterproductive terminology."

"So why do you need a gun in the first place?" she said, wincing as if painful to ask.

"Well, I shouldn't be telling all this, but I guess now it don't much matter." He inhaled and seconds later let it out. "In the joint I got in tight with the Aryan Brotherhood. Ever hear of them? For my initiation, I was supposed to go out and pop a spade, any spade. But I just couldn't do it. The Aryan philosophy I support to the max, especially defending our women. But I couldn't just flat-out shoot nobody, not even one of them."

Where in my job description does it say I have to listen to this hurtful rant?

"Well ma'am, I've been up front with you," Mike was saying, after a long pause during which she said nothing, just listened to his anxious breathing. "You asked so I'm gonna be straight with you. I did a year for auto burglary. Wired up on crystal meth like an idiot. Speed. Speed kills. Anyway, in the Marine Corps I had nothing against spades. Hey, you wanna know what USMC *really* stands for? Uncle Sam's Misguided Children. Hah-hah-hah." His voice spun out gravelly after that outburst, then climbed higher like some steroid-juiced wrestle-mania guy. "In the joint all a spade talks about is humping white chicks. And they all got AIDS. One tried to jump me in the laundry room but I jammed him up big-time. Anything white they'll jump. Got to the point I couldn't stomach'em. Animals! Hey sarge you writing all this down?"

The zip of a cigarette lighter and another bleak interval of silence. Mike said, "We got a secret plan to get rid of them, but I can't say no more about it."

She noticed the fake bravado and tremulous anger when he brought up the attacking inmate. Imagining Mike as blond and slight, she guessed that like Jeffrey Dahmer, he too was made evil by prison rape. Her own brother had served proudly in the Marines and she refused to accept that Gil and this backward criminal once wore the same uniform.

"Michael, why don't you let the lady get off the phone," Sergeant Daniels said. "Then you can call me or let me call you direct."

"It's Mike. No dice *compadre*. She leaves and I hang up. Period."

Gripping the sandwiched phones, Gwen understood she had to guard her heart against the venom spewing from this vicious mouth. She imagined Nina singing "Mississippi Goddam," about the murder of Martin Luther King and four little Birmingham girls blown up in the Sixteenth Street Baptist church. Reflected on the turns her life had taken to this moment, the great-granddaughter of slaves and sharecroppers, trying now to save a lowlife who'd hate her and those she loved if ever he spotted her round brown face.

She imagined herself a law professor using the Socratic Method, and with questions and answers leading Mike to see the folly of his awful racist beliefs. Better still, the police should storm in there and beat him silly. Send in the dogs. Drag him out by the heels.

At eight-thirty, Mike thanked her "for being so nice." Said he'd take one last call from Sergeant Daniels to see what he had to offer. She gave out her number in the event he needed to call back and immediately regretted it. Before ending the call she asked, "Will the Aryan people be angry because you didn't--didn't kill a black person?"

"Now you're talking prison politics, and that ain't healthy if I end up back in the joint."

"I see," she said.

Then he was gone, but called back thirty minutes later. Said it was raining like a banshee. Said he'd phoned his girlfriend and his best friend's mom to say good-bye in case he didn't come out alive.

"I'm sure you and Sergeant Daniels can work something out," she said, between bites on a ham and provolone sandwich, surprised by the chill in her voice.

"He keeps saying the cop ain't dead."

"I've been watching on TV and they're reporting the same thing, Mike."

"Hey, I'm not some fried-chicken-Obama-loving-spade. I was born at night but not last night."

A voice. Gwen can hear it clearly, a spirit-crushing voice vigorously mocking her belief in the innate goodness of mankind and, as the stench behind Mike's words mercifully fades away, she knows she must do something.

"Just one minute mister. There's something else you need to hear, and calling me back must be a sign from God to lay into your hide. Why--why are you such a hateful person?"   She sucked air in deeply, blood rushing to her cheeks. All fire and ice. Expanding with righteous indignation. Tense, but warily confident, as if balancing a Faberge Easter egg atop her head.

He tried to speak, but she would have none of it.

"You've been making outrageous racist comments to me, a black woman whom you clearly know nothing about." Voice rising, crackling deep in the throat, but it can't be helped. "I've had enough of your ugly talk. Don't appreciate it one bit. Do you hear me?"

The starfish is the only animal that can turn its stomach inside out—trivia picked up from who-knows-where. Now, as a wooden silence engulfed them, she imagined him scurrying, trying to turn his miserable self inside out. Trying to get away from the grime encrusting his heart.

"Really? Sorry 'bout that Miss Gwen. But what I said before got nothing to do with you or your people. Didn't see a one when I ran in here. Besides, like I said, couldn't just shoot one, couldn't do it."

Another brooding pause and she understood to give him the space to worm his way out.

"Sorry if I offended you. I mean you really didn't--you know, sound like one. But guess what? I really liked O.J. No joke. My brother had his posters on the wall, I looked up to him when I was a kid. Then he turns around and starts messing with our women. People change, you know. Weird huh?"

"Yes, people change," all she could manage through tight teeth.

"Well, I guess I'll be saying so long ma'am. And thanks for everything. Now if you could say a little prayer for me that would be really nice. Can't hurt."

She ended the call, feeling an inexplicable sense of guilt, as though a mother abandoning a newborn at the back door of a church. Turning to Sam, she told him everything, watching his eyes simmer, brow furrowing, chewing his bottom lip.

"He said all that, and me right here?"

"Thanked me too."

"Dumb-ass white boy, I hope he get every thing he deserve. I'm just saying."

She could hear her mother: *A man don't buy the cow when the milk is free.*

She waved, more tiredly than dismissive. "So who won the game?"

"You mean match? Serena." He popped another beer, and then bopped down the hall to watch TV, laughing good-naturedly about something he knew and she didn't.

Later, still in her office clothes, a coral linen suit ordered from Coldwater Creek, she glided her slippered feet down the hall and joined him to catch the ten o'clock news.

"Did we miss anything?" she asked, suddenly aware of being ruinously tired.

"Well, right now they're saying this joker wants the sergeant to come up to the store door. Says he's fixin' to come out, but first wants to meet the person he's been talking to."

"Meet?" she echoed.

"Snap! That boy is wack."

Getting late. She's ready to crash, nothing to do now but climb into bed. Catch the news in the morning. Before closing her eyes, the last thing she remembers is Sergeant Daniels' ruddy face. The police remain in contact with the suspect, he reported, sounding hopeful.

Sam leaves first in the morning so Gwen waited for him to finish knocking around in the bathroom, the other one she reserves for guests and can't-hold-it-any-longer peeing.

She padded down the hall, pausing to gently straighten the Gauguin print. Getting to the couch, she dropped down, pulled her robe together and aimed the remote. Glad to be alone.

The rain has stopped. Shimmering beaded drops roll off yellow police tape fluttering in the breeze. Small gray puddles pattern the sidewalk. Holding a microphone, a reporter had taken up a position in front of the store's entrance. He is young with light skin. His voice is high, not deep like Sam. Looking into the camera, wearing a mask of studied concern, he said the last telephone communication police had with Mike was approximately 11:00 P.M. Because they didn't know three hours later whether he was alive or had killed himself, a SWAT team entered the store and found him in the produce locker behind crates of lettuce. After he pointed a handgun, officers opened fire. Company attorney *Glenn* Hudson assisted in negotiating with the suspect, the reporter said, but all efforts to end the standoff without incident proved unsuccessful.

"What does it *prove?*" Absolutely nothing, she cried out to the uncaring air. Nothing.

The screen flashed Mike's photo from a high school yearbook. Warhol's fifteen minutes slashed to a posthumous five seconds. Struggling to tamp down tears, she regarded the loopy grin above the thin neck, the blond hair, the girly eyelashes, and didn't know whether she'd scream or sob. Something sank inside her, a sudden sickening thud far down between the heart and stomach, a delayed reaction after the spectacle of senseless death.

She needs time to process all this. The police, Mike, the male species overall, so lacking in forbearance and expressive skills the primal throbbing of their cock drives them to gun down each other. *Shooting sperm, shooting bullets, do both shots produce the same thrill?*

And she's been thinking, again, about the arc of this life with Sam—the nibbling feeling that more awaits her out there. Is he, after all, just another chest-thumping Neanderthal? Does he really believe Mike deserved to die this way?

Hazy introspection left her toying with the notion that some day she might post her own Craigslist ad. "Maybe," she told herself, "just to see what happens."

She hadn't thought it through, but if it happens, if it comes to that, the ad will reach out for a man well read and alert to the world of ideas. A man comfortable in a business suit, *sans* bling-bling, who enjoys going out and doing fun things. Turned off by hip-hop, he'll appreciate the baroque, classical and romantic periods of Bach, Beethoven and Brahms. He'll walk with himself between her and the curb on Michigan Avenue, shopping and holding hands without embarrassment along the Magnificent Mile. He'll say "invariably," instead of "nine times out of ten." He will never, ever, *axe someone* a question. And he'll take the time to show up and vote.

Sam's moving down the hall now. Those big fourteens whooshing along the carpet. In a moment, he'll sidle up for a goodbye kiss. She figures he will ask about Mike, show a little concern. But he's blissfully unconcerned. And now he's saying things in her ear, silky sweet-talk that she's only half-ready to hear. He takes her in his arms, then steps back, puzzled, hands falling away.

Don't ask, Gwen's misty eyes beseech him. Please don't.

NEGLECTED HELP

JOHN COWPER POWYS (1872-1963)

(pronounced "cooper po-is")

A great and comparatively neglected, foolishly under-rated British writer, English with a Welsh heritage—maybe too wild and Melville-like, Whitman-like for his home country; maybe too passionate, original, idea-loving, and varied for the United States: novelist, lecturer on literature, essayist, practical philosopher, humorist, visionary. An original and exciting mind. A body of work of amazing range and depth created over a career of 60 years. Prose stylist of the first rank. Long-lived prophet and clown. Major novels. Books on Hardy, Rabelais, Dostoevsky, The Pleasures of Literature. Books of useful philosophy for everyone, not for experts. All inter-related by the major themes of a rich and unusual, sensual , powerful mind.

I think it's best for my purpose here not to comment a lot more but simply to give a short list of significant works so anyone interested can see what he has to offer.

First, here's a sample: the "Table of Contents" for one of his sharp, brief, clear books of useful philosophy, *In Spite Of: A Philosophy for Everyman* (and Everywoman too—he was original there too)—

In Spite of . . .

Experts
Loneliness
Pride
Orthodoxy and Heresy
Madness
Class
Insecurity
Belief
Other People

Each of these is the topic of a chapter. This book was published in 1953 when he was 81. There are also letters, diaries, poems too: with all the rest, especially the major novels, it's a stunning achievement.

Here's the short list promised.

Some major novels (there may be other "major" ones, there's a total of about 13—things are still a little uncertain):

> *Wolf Solent*, 1929
> *A Glastonbury Romance*, 1932
> *Weymoth Sands*, 1934
> *Maiden Castle*, 1936

Some practical philosophy:

> *The Art of Happiness*, 1923
> *In Defense of Sensuality*, 1930
> *A Philosophy of Solitude*, 1933
> *In Spite Of*, 1953

Some literary studies (he made his living as a lecturer on literature in America for some 25 years, 1905-1930)

> *Visions and Revisions*, 1915
> *One Hundred Best Books*, 1916
> *The Meaning of Culture*, 1929

The wild, wonderful, profound "revolution" of the

> *Autobiography*, 1934

Here's a lot to enjoy and learn from. A book can change your life, right?

GG

CONTRIBUTORS

NATALIA BARB, twenty, is a lifetime resident of Emporia, KS. Natalia's interest in writing was born of an abiding love for books she gained as a child while her father read Tolkien aloud. From her mother, third-generation Hispanic and first in her family to achieve a college degree, she learned that words were vessels: vehicles for idea and change. Recently, Natalia married and is currently attending Emporia State University majoring in Literature.

MATTHEW M. CARIELLO lives in Bexley, Ohio, and teaches in the English Department at the Ohio State University. His poetry has been published in *Poet Lore, Artful Dodge, The Journal of New Jersey Poets, Frogpond, Acorn, Simply Haiku, Riverbed, The Heron's Nest* and *Modern Haiku.* His reviews and fiction have appeared in *The Indiana Review, The Journal, The Long Story, Iron Horse Literary Review, Parting Gifts,* and *Ohioana.*

MARTIN ELWELL is a native New Englander currently living outside of Chicago. He has a degree in English Literature from Colby College and an MFA in Poetry from Lesley University. He is actively contemplating a move back to New England as well as other random wanderings.

MYLES GORDON is a humanities teacher in the Boston school system through the Boston Teacher Residency. A past honorable mention for the AWP Intro Award, Myles is also a past winner of the Grolier Poetry Prize. He has published poems in several small, literary magazines, and in the anthology *Awake! A Reader for the Sleepless* (Soft Skull Press). A former television producer for Boston's ABC Network affiliate, WCVB TV, he is the winner of four New England Emmy Awards for producing and writing. He co-produced the independent documentary: *Touching Lives: Portraits of Deafblind People*, which premiered at Boston's Museum of Fine Arts.

R.E. HAYES is a writer who was born and raised in Chicago. He joined the Marines after high school and served four years in the infantry. Formerly a federal labor lawyer, he was educated at Indiana University, Bloomington.

DIANE LEFER'S most recent book, *California Transit* (Sarabande 2007) received the Mary McCarthy Prize in Short Fiction. She lives in Los Angeles where she has been a volunteer interpreter for immigrants in detention and has led creative writing workshops for adjudicated youth and kids in the foster-care system. Her ongoing collaboration with exiled Colombian theatre artist

Hector Aristizábal encompasses work for the page and the stage as well as social action workshops.

Lucia P. May is a poet and violinist who teaches and plays in St. Paul, MN. She is a longtime arts advocate for various major arts and educational institutions. Lucia's work has appeared or will appear in *Main Channel Voices* and the *Evening Street Review*. She is a finalist in Winning Writers' War Poetry Contest and was a finalist in the 2009 Loft Mentorship Program.

Peter Mladinic teaches at New Mexico Junior College and has had poems published in numerous literary magazines including the *American Literary Review*, *Poetry Northwest*, and *Poetry East*. His book, *Lost in Lea*, was published in 2008 by the Lea County Museum Press.

Jane Sadek chased the American Dream up and down the corporate ladder, until she decided to hang up her business suit and take out a pen. Now she spends her days writing poetry, short stories, and creative non-fiction, while laboring on her first novel. Jane recently earned a BA in Art & Performance at The University of Texas at Dallas, graduating Magna Cum Laude with Major Honors. Visit her on the Web at www.JaneSadek.com.

Michael Salcman's poems appear in *Alaska Quarterly Review, Hopkins Review, New Letters, Ontario Review, Harvard Review, Raritan, Notre Dame Review*, and *New York Quarterly*. He is the author of four chapbooks, most recently, *Stones In Our Pockets* (Parallel Press). His collection *The Clock Made of Confetti* (Orchises), was nominated for The Poets' Prize in 2009 and was a Finalist for The Towson University Prize in Literature. He is a neurosurgeon and art critic in Baltimore.

Stephanie Silvia was born in Brooklyn, where she taught public school after years of directing stephanie silvia:NORTH/SOUTH Dance, a modern company in New York City. She received an MFA from the University of North Carolina at Greensboro and attended school in Boston and San Francisco. Her poetry, reviews and articles have been published in the *Northcoast Journal, The Times Standard*, (Eureka CA), *College of the Redwoods Writers and Poets, The Cherry Blossom Review, Elephant* and in the anthology, *Women.Period.*, (Spinster's Ink Press). Stephanie is a student of Diane di Prima.

Lianne Spidel is a former high school English teacher who lives and writes in Greenville, Ohio, and is a member of a local writing group, The Greenville

Poets. Her work is current or forthcoming in *Hawaii Pacific Review*, *Oracle*, *Cloudbank* and *Xanadu*. Her chapbook of art poems, *Chrome*, was published in 2006 by Finishing Line Press.

Adam Sturtevant is a 26-year-old writer and musician living in Brooklyn, New York. As a drummer, he has performed with many different indie artists, most notably St. Vincent, Via Audio, and Sufjan Stevens. His fiction has appeared in *Decomp Magazine*, *Two Hawks Quarterly*, and recently won third place in the 2009 Santa Fe Writers Project Literary Awards.

Paula Anne Yup first published in a magazine entitled "CQ" after encouragement from editor Dr. Kenneth Atchity who taught at Occidental College where Paula spent her undergraduate years. After over eight hundred submissions she has had poems published in The Third Woman: Minority Women Writers of the United States, Passages North Anthology, What Book!?, Outrider Press anthologies and other places. She has an MFA in poetry from Vermont College in Montpelier, Vermont. She has had extended visits to Tokyo and the Baja, and now lives in the Republic of the Marshall Islands.

Mary Zelinka is the Advocacy Services Manager at the Center Against Rape and Domestic Violence in Corvallis, Oregon where she gets to witness the remarkable strength and resiliency of survivors of sexual and domestic violence every day. She has been involved in the movement to end violence against women since 1980. Her writing has appeared in *CALYX*, *Open Spaces*, and *The Sun*.